Not Broken

Lisamarie Kade

Because sometimes we all need a little sunshine to
drive out the grumpy thoughts.

While this is not a dark romance book, this story
mentions kidnapping, physical assault, sexual
assault, death.
Please proceed with caution.

Chapter One

Finnley

I check myself once more in the visor mirror. Freckles dance across my cheekbones. The setting sun hits my red curls just right. It makes them look as if they are glowing. I swipe my hair over my shoulder and climb out of my Camaro.

I'm excited about tonight. I have a date. First dates are always hard, but I've been talking to Tyler for two months now and feel good about meeting him.

We met on a dating app and hit it off right away. That's not usually the case.

See, I know what I'm looking for in a relationship and will not lower my standards. I know my worth and I'm almost certain that Tyler is what I'm looking for.

It doesn't hurt that he has dreamy blue eyes,

dark hair, and a smile that belongs on the cover of a magazine.

Taking the steps up to the Iron Rose, an Irish pub, I notice a few officers. By the time I reach the podium, there are several more. Some are even talking to people that are seated.

"Hi there! How many?" the petite hostess asks.

"Um, two. Is everything okay?" I nod toward a few officers.

"Oh them, yeah, it's our annual dine with a cop night. They are serving guests all night. Whatever tips they receive goes back into the community." She smiles big as she walks me to my booth. "Here ya go, enjoy."

"Thanks. Oh, I'm expecting someone to join me."

"Sure thing, what's your name?"

"Finnley."

"Got it. Your server should be with you shortly."

I smile as she walks away. It's not long before an officer walks up to my table. Not just any officer either. The man is gorgeous. Like it should be a crime, he looks that good. He oozes sex.

"Hi, I'm Officer Hayworth and I will be your server tonight for the Dine with a Cop Event."

Hot damn, even his voice screams sex.

"Hi." It's the only word I manage to get out.

"So, what can I get you to drink?"

"I'll take a Malibu Bay Breeze."

"Sure thing. I see someone else is joining you." He nods to the menu that is laid out across from me. "I'll check back in a few."

Tyler. Shit. I was so caught up in this good looking cop that I forgot I was meeting a date.

"That'll be great. Thanks."

The officer whose name I have already forgotten smiles before walking off. Thank goodness because he is quite the distraction. I won't lie. From his dark hair, which is styled perfectly, to his ocean blue eyes. I could get lost at sea just looking at them. I can tell he is packing solid muscle too. Just by the way the black uniform hugs his body.

I shake my head and laugh. What is wrong with me? I'm about to meet my date any minute and I'm busy checking out some other guy.

The officer returns promptly with my drink and sets it down in front of me.

"Here you go. I'll check back in a few." The second he is gone, I reach for my drink. It tastes amazing, just the right amount of pineapple and cranberry juice. Topped with a lot of rum.

I decide to pull out my phone to waste time while waiting on Tyler. He lives about forty-five minutes away. I'm only about ten, fifteen tops from the Iron Rose. That is one of the perks of living in the city. I love it too. I enjoy the hustle and noise. I love the night life, and pretty much everything that comes with city living.

"Would you like another?" That deep voice startles me, causing me to look down at my now empty glass. I didn't realize I finished it.

"Yes, please."

This time, he only nods before turning to go. I don't mind it, because I get to watch his ass as he goes.

I glance back at my phone to check the time. I know Tyler has a bit of drive, but I feel like he should have been here by now. I hope everything is all right. Slight panic grows. What if he stood me up? What if he saw me and decided to run? I have sent him numerous photos. He knows what I look like. I've even sent him photos of me at the gym with my red hair all frizzy and unruly.

When the officer comes back with my drink, I take it from him before he can set it down on the table.

"Feisty," he says, and I nearly spit the liquid back into my cup.

"Excuse me?"

Those blue eyes find mine.

"Sorry, sorry." He laughs. "You seemed eager for that drink. Is everything okay?"

Great. Now I feel stupid, and he probably thinks I'm an alcoholic.

"Yes, I'm sorry. I'm waiting for my date to arrive."

"Ah, I see."

I watch as the gorgeous officer in front of me rubs his jaw. He has light stubble starting along the jawline. I take another sip to distract myself from staring at him because I won't lie. He is nice to stare at.

"He's most likely stuck in traffic. I'll check back in a few unless you want me to put in an appetizer."

I shake my head. "I'm good. Thank you, though."

Tyler should be here, even with traffic. I unlock my phone and open the dating app, but there are no new messages from him.

I even check my text messages. Nothing. I get up and go over to the hostess stand. Maybe the hostess seated him and forgot to tell him I had a seat. That must be it.

"Excuse me, I'm supposed to be meeting someone here. His name is Tyler. Did anyone come in and mention the name Finnley?"

The two women standing there share a look. And not a good one. The petite one, the same person who seated me, casts her eyes down. The other, who has beautiful blonde hair and almond eyes, gives me a sad smile.

"What?" I finally ask, unable to take anymore awkward silence.

"A man did come in. He looked around, mentioned your name, and then took off before I could respond."

"He was here?"

The petite woman nods. "I'm sorry."

Great.

I was stood up. How fucking great.

Walking back to my table, I flag the officer who has been serving me down. I need a damn drink.

"Hey, did your date—"

I shake my head. "Don't ask. Just bring me another drink."

"Umm, are you sure?"

"I said bring me another drink. Please."

He nods and quickly walks away.

Gosh, I sound like a bitch. It's not his fault, but for fuck's sake why didn't Tyler stay? Did he catch sight of me while looking around and thought my red hair was too much? What if I was too chubby for him? I glance down at myself. I'm a curvy woman with thick thighs. I am big-chested. There is no hiding the babes. Yes, that's what I call my boobs.

Tyler knows all this though. I have sent him numerous photos of myself. I don't play the catfish game. I'm confident in my skin. I have never been ashamed and love my body just the way it is.

So why did he bail? It doesn't make any sense.

I open the dating app and send a quick message.

> Hey, are we still meeting?

I decide to play it cool. He doesn't know that I know he bailed. I just can't put it together. If he decided I'm not worthy, that's on him. Playing games is shitty. I don't have time for high school drama. Really. The least he can do is be honest. Give me closure.

The officer comes back with my drink and sets it down in front of me.

"This one is on the house." He winks.

He just winked at me. This smoking hot cop just winked at me.

"What's your name again?" I ask as I reach for my drink. I take a long sip. Getting drunk sounds good right now.

"Hayworth. Brett Hayworth. And you are?"

"Since when do servers ask for names?"

Yup, it has been confirmed, I am a complete bitch.

"You have a good point. However, I'm not your average server. I'm a cop and there is a good chance one of us here will end up pulling you over later for driving while intoxicated."

He gives his best megawatt smile. One that would make any girl drop to her knees.

"My name is Finnley."

"It's nice to meet you, Finnley." The way he says my name makes my heart skip a beat. His sultry voice is inviting.

"Would you like anything else? Food perhaps?"

I glance down at my glass. It's empty. That was fast. When the hell did I finish it? I look up at Officer Hayworth. Those piercing blue eyes of his stare back at me. Eyes that don't judge me.

"I'd like another drink. I'll go ahead and order." While waiting, I looked over the menu. I already know what I want.

"What would you like?"

"I'll have the eight-ounce steak. Medium rare."

"Medium rare?" He quirks an eyebrow at me in question.

I laugh and toss a few curls over my shoulder. "Yes. No one seems to know how to cook a steak the right way so I'm hoping if I say medium rare, it'll come out medium and not burnt to a crisp."

The man in front of me tilts his head back and laughs. Straight up laughs at my words. I cross my arms across my chest.

"I'm sorry, sorry," he says through laughter. "I take it you have had a few bad steaks."

"Too many to count, but yet here I am ordering one in hopes that this time will be different."

"I'll make sure the chef knows to cook it right. What sides would you like?"

"Broccoli and a side salad. Ranch."

"You got it. I'll be back with another Malibu Bay Breeze."

"Thanks, Brett."

He gives me a surprised look. I just smile. I used his first name, and he wasn't expecting it.

"By the way, there's not a chance in hell you or anyone else in uniform will be pulling me over. I am not that stupid." I wink.

I might as well flirt and have a little fun tonight.

Chapter Two

Finnley

Now that my food has arrived, Brett is nowhere to be found, and I am in desperate need of some ranch. He's probably avoiding me. He probably thinks I am a sad, pathetic chick that got stood up. What's worse is people here know I was stood up. There's a good chance it's being gossiped about in the back. This is embarrassing. To be stood up is one thing, but to be stood up and other people witnessing it takes it to another level.

This disaster of a night can't end fast enough.

As soon as I see an officer, I wave him down. I don't care that it's not Brett.

"Hi, I'm not sure where my cop is, wait, that came out wrong." I slap my forehead. "The cop that was serving me, I haven't seen him and would like some ranch."

This cop smiles. His blonde hair is cut short, military style. He's hot too, though not nearly as hot as Brett.

"I'll let him know. I think he's in the back."

I cringe internally. Yeah, probably in the back listening to the gossip. "Thanks."

Mr. Blonde Cop disappears, and I am left alone with my thoughts. It's fine, I tell myself. Perfectly fine. I do not care if these strangers talk about it. They don't know me. I don't know them.

After giving myself that little pep talk, I decide to check my phone for the hundredth time. As soon as I unlock it, Brett walks up with the ranch.

"How's everything taste? Steak cooked just right?"

"It is."

"Anything else I can get for you?"

"Another drink, please," I demand.

Officer Brett's eyes narrow as they meet mine. He wants to say something. I can see it written all over his face.

He doesn't.

Instead, he turns and walks away without saying a single word. I'm curious to know what he was going to say. It might be the rum taking over, which I'll gladly allow to happen. If it takes away this feeling of rejection for a little while, I'm all for it.

When Mr. Blue Eyes returns, I give my best seductive smile.

"Tell me something about you." I catch him off guard

"Uh, what do you want to know?" He gives me a questioning look.

"Anything, like are you married? Do you have a girlfriend?"

I hope that's a no to both because that would damper my flirtatious mood.

His lips press into a thin line. "No longer married."

Ah, I have hit a sensitive subject. Brett's entire demeanor has changed and not in a good way.

"I'm sorry," I say as I reach out and rub his arm. I wink once. "Or maybe I'm not." I'm definitely tipsy, saying something wild like that.

He yanks his arm back. "Finnley," he warns.

"What? I'm just being honest. Maybe I want to get to know you a little better."

"You're drunk."

"Tipsy, not drunk," I correct, pointing a finger at him.

"Tipsy? Tipsy enough to start flirting with me."

"So?"

Brett tips his head back and laughs a little. "If you were sober, would you be flirting?"

I think about his question for a second. Would I? Absolutely. I am a single woman and was stood up by a guy. I sure as hell would still flit. The man is hot as sin.

"I would."

"Is that so?"

I nod while taking a sip of my drink. "I'm single, there is nothing wrong with flirting."

"My turn to ask a question."

"Ask away, Officer."

Brett rubs his chin. I don't miss the way his eyes skim over my body, from the top of my head down to my legs. I notice.

"Why didn't your date show?"

Shit.

I wasn't expecting him to ask about that. I was banking on him flirting with me back. I reach for my glass and down the rest of the contents.

When I set the glass down, I look Brett straight into his ocean blue eyes.

"He stood me up."

His expression morphs into something serious, and he stands taller, nodding as if he understands.

And just like that, the flirting flies right out of the window. I shrug my shoulder and dip my broccoli into the ranch. I silently curse myself for being honest. I should have lied and kept flirting.

Brett reaches for my empty glass. "Can I get you anything?"

"Another drink would be great."

"How are you getting home?"

Home. Well damn, I didn't think about that. I drove myself. I wasn't planning on drinking like this.

"That's what I thought. I'll bring you a water."

"What? No, it's fine. I'll just call an Uber or something."

"An Uber or something? You want a stranger to drive you home?" His demeanor has completely changed. His expression is one that I can't quite read, but I'm thinking he's unhappy with me.

Not particularly, but it's all I have to work with. I don't say that bit out loud. No way will I let this man think I can't handle life on my own. I do it every single day.

"I'm not fragile. I will be fine."

"Fine. Whatever."

I stare at Brett's fine ass as he stomps his way to the bar. He's pissed. Why though? I'm not sure. He doesn't know me. What does he care if I let a stranger take me home?

Brett does not return with my drink. No, Mr. Blonde Cop comes back with my Malibu Bay Breeze. What the fuck?

"Brett's a little tied up in the back. He asked me to bring this out for you."

"Thanks," I mumble through clenched teeth.

Busy my ass. He is avoiding me.

"Seems you struck a chord with him. I don't know what you said or did, but he's fired up." He laughs as he sets my drink down. "Whatever you did, keep it up."

So my drinking and possibly getting in a vehicle with a stranger has him all pissy? Interesting.

I'm not sure how much time passes before Brett comes back with my check in hand. He doesn't smile and those piercing blue eyes of his are throwing daggers my way.

"My time here is up. Here is your check, no rush though. Order another drink or ten."

Ouch.

"Are you always so grumpy?"

"I'm not grumpy. You are being foolish and stubborn."

I smile at him before taking one final sip of my delicious drink. "What do you care how I get home? As long as I'm not behind the wheel driving, it should not matter to you."

"You are right. I couldn't care less. One of the servers that work here will be by shortly to take care of you. Have a wonderful night, *Finnley*."

The way he spits my name out sends chills down my spine. I immediately stand to my feet and nearly stumble. Brett grabs my upper arm, steadying me.

A giggle escapes my lips. "Look at you being a hero cop, trying to save me."

"Finnley," Brett warns, but I'm too busy

looking at where his hand meets my arm. He grips me firmly. I like it.

"Are you one of those guys who is rough in bed?"

He immediately drops his hand. Shock evident on his face. "You are drunk."

I can't help but laugh. I am.

Reaching into my purse, I pull out enough cash to cover my tab and leave a decent tip. Drunk or not, I know to leave a decent tip.

I gather my things and realize Brett is still standing there. Is he waiting on me?

"You are still here?" I say, raising an eyebrow.

The gorgeous man in front of me turns and walks off without so much as a word.

He is no fun.

Chapter Three

Brett

Damn that fiery redhead. I curse as I storm out of the Iron Rose and head for my cruiser. I start it but don't put it in gear. I don't have it in me to pull out of this parking lot. Not without making sure Finnley has a sober ride home. She has me too wound up. I haven't let anyone get under my skin.

Not since Abigail.

Not since my brother.

So why the fuck am I letting some stranger get under my skin? Fuck if I know. I hit the air conditioner, turning it up. I need to cool down.

I tell myself it's because she looked so damn sad waiting on her date. Dude never showed and it clearly crushed her.

Again, that is not my problem. Not one damn

bit. Why people date these days is mind-blowing. No one is honest and everyone is sneaky as hell. Like my brother and Abigail. I'm not bitter. Disappointed, yes. Bitter, no. I expected the woman I loved to be upfront and honest. To be faithful. What I didn't expect was for her to be having an affair with my younger brother.

Fuck it, I'm bitter.

It's been three years since I found out and I'm over it most days. Days like today though, when I see someone with relationship issues, it gets under my skin. Sure, I see it weekly when I go on domestic calls and all that, but that is not the same. I am in work mode.

I catch sight of her red hair as I stare in the rearview mirror. I follow her movements and see her walk up to a black Chevy Camaro. There's no fucking way she is going to drive out of here.

No fucking way.

I throw my cruiser in reverse fast and speed off toward her shiny sports car, throwing it in park directly behind her. If she thinks she is going to leave, she'll have to take out my vehicle first.

I get out fully prepared to rip her apart, except when I walk up to the car, I hear her voice. The windows are cracked, and the sunroof is open. She is singing loudly and way off tune. She is singing some girly shit. At least I think it is girly.

I almost laugh until I remember she is intoxicated and in her vehicle. I walk up and knock on the driver window.

Finnley surprises me once again when she pops out of the backseat of the passenger side.

"Hi there, Brett!" she says loudly, like she is excited.

"What are you doing?"

"Chillin', want to join me?"

"No. What are you doing in your car?"

"I told you, I am chillin'."

"Finnley, you know I cannot let you drive out of here, right?"

"I'm not driving anywhere, silly. Didn't you see me get out of the back seat?"

"Well, yes, I did."

"Okay, so, I can't drive from the back seat. Like I said, I'm chillin'."

"Where are your keys?"

She laughs as she hitches a finger toward the trunk.

"Your keys are in your trunk?" I ask, eyebrow raised.

"They sure are, along with my purse."

She really is something. A spitfire.

"And just what is your plan? You gonna sleep out here?"

"Yeah, you know, I got to thinking about what

you said about letting a stranger drive me home and figured this would be the safer of the two. I figured it might be fun to camp in my car." She giggles, causing a little piece of ice to chip off of my cold heart. No way can I let her sleep out here in a damn parking lot.

"You can leave now. I'm not in distress. I'm sure your services are needed elsewhere."

Her and her damn smart mouth. She gets under my skin.

"Don't think about driving out of here. I'll be letting the others know the description of your car."

She waves me off. "Oh please. I'm drunk, not stupid. Maybe if I'm lucky, the next cop I come across will be just as hot but not as much of an asshole." She climbs back into her back seat, shutting the door.

I storm back to my cruiser and climb in. She wants to sit and bake in the Florida heat, fine with me. Not my fucking problem. Even after dark it is still in the high eighties. She can suffer for all I care.

I grab the radio to put out a heads up on her sports car but stop short. I can't let her stay here all night, can I?

I can so why am I hesitating on radioing in the description of her car?

"Fuck!" I spit out as I climb back out of my cruiser and head back to her car.

This time I walk up to the passenger side of her Camaro and yank on the handle of the back door. It opens right up. She didn't even lock it. There she lays across the backseat with her arm across her forehead.

What the hell is wrong with her?!

"Hey!" Finnley shouts as she sits up. "Oh, it's just you."

She plops back against the seat and closes her eyes. Her red curls fan around her face. From here, it is hard to see the freckles on her cheeks. I know they are there though. I studied them enough tonight.

Dude, what the hell is wrong with me? That's the million dollar question of the night. Before I can stop myself, I'm blurting words out. "Come on, I'll just drive you home."

She lays there unmoving. For a moment I wonder if she has passed out. I watch as her chest rises and falls evenly. The last thing I want to do is babysit a drunk chick tonight and yet here I am.

"Finnley."

"What, Officer?" She sits up and pushes the curls away from her face. She looks so innocent, even though I have a feeling she is anything but.

"I said I'll drive you home."

"Okay, let me just grab my purse."

Shaking my head, I back up just enough to give her room to get by. We almost touch. Almost. She smells like vanilla. Vanilla and rum. I watch her bend over in her trunk and try as I might, I can't seem to peel my eyes from her ass.

I have a feeling this is going to be the longest drive of my life.

Chapter Four

Finnley

"Are you coming?"

"Yeah, yeah, I just, I am worried about leaving Onyx."

"Onyx? Who the hell is Onyx?"

I giggle as Brett glances around as if someone is going to pop out. "Silly man, Onyx is my Camero."

The man in front of me glares at me. I bet he wishes his eyes alone could shoot a dagger straight through my heart. It makes me laugh more.

Brett shakes his head in disbelief. "Come on, Finnley, I'll drive you home and you can figure out picking up your car tomorrow." His deep voice sounds sincere. I know I am driving his last damn nerve. Or maybe he's just acting like he holds some authority over me. Just like my dad did when he wanted me to follow the rules as a teenager. I'll show him I can follow his rules.

I pop up and gather my things. When I get out of my back seat a little too fast, I sway on my feet. Brett reaches out quickly, grabbing my hips. He steadies me, but I feel it. The heat from his touch. He must feel it as well because his fingers linger a beat too long.

"Let's go." Stern words leave his mouth as he lets me go, forcing his arms to his sides. I follow behind him as we slowly make our way to his SUV. I am not going to lie, I'm sort of excited. I've never been in a cop car before. The feeling of being a bad girl runs through my veins. I think I like it.

Brett opens the front passenger door and gestures for me to get in.

"What's this? Not going to punish me and put me in the back seat?" I can't help myself as the words slip out.

"Finnley, if I am putting you in any back seat with the sole purpose of punishing you, it will not be the back seat of my cruiser." There's a tic in his jaw as he waits for me to make my move. Hot damn, if that man's words didn't just turn me on. I cannot make my feet move. His words have me frozen in place. Dirty thoughts swirl in my mind.

"Get in."

This time I do as I'm told. I climb in and before Brett can shut the door, I decide to ask him a daring question. "Would you like to punish me, Officer? Because I might like that."

The man runs a hand through his dark hair. He says nothing while shaking his head. He shuts the door, effectively ending the conversation without giving me an answer. What a buzz kill.

When he gets in, he does not make eye contact with me. He just puts the vehicle in drive.

We drive in silence for what feels like forever when really it's probably only a few minutes. I can't take it anymore though. The silence is suffocating.

"So," I giggle, "where are we going?" I haven't given him my address, yet here we are driving.

"I told you, I'm taking you home." A sigh leaves his lips. He sounds annoyed. That's not my fault though. I was perfectly fine sleeping off my drunkenness in Onyx.

"I haven't given you my address."

"You didn't have to. I ran the tag on your car. I'm assuming you are still in the apartments on Hawthorne Way?"

Okay, that was both slick and kind of hot.

"That's me."

"Figured."

He sounds so unfazed while I am sitting over here all hot and bothered as I study him. I'm no longer sad about being stood up. This is way better.

All I can think about is the way his arm muscles flex as he grips the steering wheel. It might be the alcohol, but something in the air has shifted. I feel it.

I know we're coming up on my complex. If I'm going to make a move, I need to do it like yesterday.

"Brett." I pause to carefully choose my words. "Are you off shift now?"

"For the remainder of the night." He casts a sideways glance my way.

"How old are you?"

"I turned thirty last month."

"It's a shame we didn't know each other then. We could have celebrated."

"We don't know each other now." It's all he says.

"We're getting there," I say, hoping to turn this convo back around.

"You are drunk, Finnley."

"Only a little. That doesn't mean anything."

"It means everything."

Brett shakes his head as he turns into my complex. He pulls up to the gate box and before I can rattle off my code, he enters a number and up the gate goes. It's like magic. He most likely knows the code because he is a cop. See, not that drunk.

He continues driving through the complex, even though I haven't told him which direction my apartment is. Probably another one of his cop secrets. Even still, the thought has me feeling all sorts of ways.

Not even a minute later, Brett pulls into an empty parking spot directly in front of my apartment. He shifts the SUV into park but doesn't look my way.

"We have arrived," he replies as if I have no clue.

"I can see that, Officer. I'm not blind."

"Not blind, just drunk."

"Only a little."

"Whatever. Will you be able to make it the five hundred or so feet to your door?" he asks sarcastically while leaning back to look at me.

I lean over the console toward him. "You know, I like it when you are a little feisty. It keeps things interesting."

Brett's eyes land on my cleavage, only for a second. I smirk and he knows I caught him. It gives me all the fuel I need.

I lean up further to where my face is now inches from his. I can smell him. All woodsy like.

"Finnley," Brett warns, yet I do not listen. Instead, I make a move to kiss him.

I don't know how he does it, but he sure is fast. He is out of his SUV and rounding the front of it, coming to my side.

"Finnley, let's go." He holds his hand out for me to take. I study it for a few seconds as embarrassment threatens to flood me. I refuse to let it though. So what, he denied me a kiss.

I finally place my hand into his, allowing him

to pull me along. He quietly but swiftly walks me up to my door.

I smile. "Are you sure I can't invite you in?" Yeah, I sound foolish. I don't care though because I am horny, and this man could be the answer to the needs I currently have.

"No." Brett's words are firm, letting me know I have zero chance.

"Fine, you are no fun."

Once I have the door unlocked, I push it open and walk in. I turn to face him while leaning my head on the edge of the door.

"Is it the red hair?"

"What?" he asks, clearly confused.

"My hair, it's the hair, isn't it?" Believe it or not, some of the losers I've dated have blamed my hair on our breakup.

"No, it's not the hair. You are drunk. What kind of man would I be if I accepted your advances while you're drunk?"

Well damn, when he says it like that.

"Go to bed, Finnley, and lock the damn door."

I nod and close the door, locking it. Before I head to my room, I pause at my front window. Brett is already back in his SUV. That's not what gets me though. It's seeing him sitting in the driver seat with his head resting on the steering wheel.

Maybe, just maybe, I got to him as much as he got to me.

Chapter Five

Brett

The entire drive home I curse her. That fiery redhead got under my skin. I don't know how I let her get to me. No one gets to me. Not even the people I end up escorting to jail.

I no longer feel. Not one damn thing. Yet tonight, Finnley had me feeling some sort of bullshit. It's as if I have this pent-up energy and not a damn clue as to how to release it.

Yes, you do.

Shaking my head, I try to tell myself that it's because I felt bad for the girl. She got stood up and rumors from the back of the restaurant were that the dude walked in, got a glance, and took off fast. Not sure why. Finnley is attractive. She has curves and an ass that's nice to look at.

I need a cold shower, I decide as soon as I close

the front door behind me. Yes, a cold shower will erase all thoughts of Finnley. Especially the way she was laid out in the back seat of her sports car. Good thing I will probably never see her again. She's every bit of beautiful.

Turning the shower on, I decide against the cold shower. I strip out of my uniform and step under the spray. Hot water pours over me, and it helps me relax a little. I grab the body wash and start lathering up, but thoughts of Finnley's mouth plague my mind. My cock twitches, betraying me.

Without thinking, I grab ahold of it. I don't dare stroke it. I squeeze my cock instead.

"Fuck," I groan out in frustration.

I will not masturbate to thoughts of a stranger.

I will not masturbate to the beauty with eyes that can only be compared to the sun shining through a forest. The perfect combo of green and gold.

Against my better judgement, I stroke myself a few times. The sensation feels good, too good. Before I realize what's happening, I'm pumping harder, faster. My balls begin to tighten as I imagine what her red lips would look like wrapped around my cock.

Suddenly an image of Abigail flashes through my mind. My movements falter as I try to picture Finnley. Instead though, images of me walking in on my ex-wife with another man consume my mind. Reminding me that just thinking about another woman is pointless.

Throwing my head back, I release my cock.

I will not fucking masturbate to Finnley Thompson, especially when images of Abigail plague my mind.

Fuck.

* * *

The crack between my curtains allows just enough sun in. I roll over, hoping to fall back asleep. Sleep doesn't come.

Throwing the black sheet back, I sit up and run my hand over my face. What a rough night. I denied myself pleasure as a reminder of the pain that Abigail put me through. Do I regret it?

I'm not sure.

Maybe.

My stomach growls, reminding me of the one thing I am certain of.

Hunger.

Breakfast calls so I head out to the kitchen. This I can control.

Once the eggs and sausage are finished, I scoop them onto my plate and pour some orange juice. I consider myself healthy. I eat well and work out several times a week. Doing what I do, it is essential to be in shape.

I unlock my phone as I take the first bite. These fuckers. My phone has blown up with texts from the guys I was on shift with last night.

The first one is from Luke. I open it and immediately curse under my breath. What a fucker.

In my inbox sits a meme about getting laid followed by, "Yo, tight ass, I hope you screwed her brains out."

I should have expected this from him. Last night he kept poking at me about shacking up with her. I ignored every jab and gave no indication that I was even remotely interested in her.

I'm not.

Finnley is beautiful. Stunning. Regardless of those facts, I am not interested. I am not interested in the idea of a relationship. Not even a one night stand. Nope.

Chapter Six

Finnley

My head is pounding and thoughts of last night are a little fuzzy. I remember being at the Iron Rose and my date not showing up.

Throwing the comforter back, I stretch. Even my muscles hurt like I did something wild. Did I?

It hits me. All at once my memory comes back.

The Malibu Bay Breezes— too many to count.

The flirting with a cop and completely failing. What was his name again? I groan out loud. I cannot for the life of me remember his name. He was hot. That much I remember.

Shaking the thoughts, I tell myself it doesn't matter what his name is. I need two things. The bathroom and pain reliever. My bladder, along with my head, are about to explode.

Three hours later I am finally feeling somewhat human. The headache is gone, and I no longer look like death in my crop top and sweats. I may not be wearing makeup, but at least I am functioning.

Sighing, I check my phone again to see if the Uber driver has arrived. I am anxious and feel like a moron. I have never left Onyx anywhere, much less a damn restaurant parking lot. I should have stayed in my car; instead in my drunken state, I allowed Mr. Hot Cop to convince me to go with him. The worst part was I didn't even woo him enough for sex.

The second we pull up to my sports car, I pay and hop out. The driver starts to speak, but I close the door before I can hear what she has to say.

Walking around my entire car, I check for any signs of damage. When I reach my driver side, a little white card catches my eye. There it sits snug against my window between the rubber and glass. I pull it out and flip it over.

A sheriff's card.

Deputy Brett Hayworth.

So that was his name.

Why would he leave his card for me? That is the million dollar question. A cell number is listed underneath his name. Does he want me to call him? There is no way. He seemed very annoyed to have to deal with me last night. At least from what I remember anyway.

Unlocking my door, I slide in. "I'm sorry for leaving you here. That will not happen again." Yes, I talk to my car. It is my pride and joy. I have worked my ass off for my dream car.

Before I start Onyx up, I look at the card in my lap as if it is burning a hole in my black sweats. I have this wild urge to text the number on it. Just to see if Brett responds. Okay, it might be more stupid than wild, but I decide to do it anyway. What can I say, I like to live on the edge sometimes.

> Thanks for the ride home last night

I hit send before I talk myself into deleting it and start my car. She has a mean purr as she roars to life. Without waiting for a reply, I make my way out of this parking spot and back home. My comfy bed calls.

My phone dings while I'm driving home. I refuse to look at it while driving though. I force myself to wait until I climb into bed and unlock my phone. I click on the text and open it.

> How the hell did you get this number?

Brett's text puzzles me. How did I get his number? Does he not remember putting the card on my car? Is he dumb or does he suffer from some sort of memory loss?

> You left it on my car silly

> No I did not

That is odd. I scratch my forehead. He had to have put the card there. Who else would put his own card there? I take a photo of it and send it to him.

> I guess it magically appeared on my car

I can't help but giggle after I hit send. I know it will

probably drive him mad. I almost wish I could see his face as he opens that text.

While enjoying our back-and-forth texts, a notification sounds from my dating app.

Tyler's name appears.

Throwing my head back, I groan in frustration. He never responded last night. He for real stood me up. He probably spent all day coming up with some lame excuse. Well, let's hear it.

Hey

He sent me one word. No explanation. He better give one. Otherwise, he is getting blocked.

What?

I am really sorry about last night. Something came up and I have been tied up since.

Okay

Please forgive me. I would like to make it up to you. Let me take you out again.

I chew on my cheek for a minute while trying to debate my response. Tyler is a liar. He must think he is smooth. I am far from naive. He came last night, saw me, and left. Now he wants to gaslight me.

> No thanks. You showed your face and left without a word.

> You saw me?

> I did

> Look, I can explain.

> Then explain instead of lying

I grab for my bottle of water and take a sip. I really should not be entertaining this guy. Except there is a part of me that wants to know his reasoning. I thought we had a connection. I was excited for our date and to finally meet him in person.

I wait a few minutes. And then I wait a little longer. Tyler does not respond.

I exit the damn dating app and realize that Brett never responded either.

What the hell?

Chapter Seven

Finnley

I throw my head back in laughter. Violet tells the best stories, especially when it involves guys and how dramatic they can be. Her current flavor of the month has a man cold. She couldn't take one more minute in the house with his needy ass so here we are.

My best friend sits across from me in the booth at the Iron Rose. Yup, I returned. I have no shame. Tonight however, I will not be getting drunk. I'm drinking water.

"So, no word back from the dating app guy?" Violet raises an eyebrow. Her vibrant rainbow-colored hair is styled perfectly. Not a strand is out of place. It is the exact opposite of my red and wild curls.

"Nope, he said he could explain. I told him to go ahead. I wanted to see what excuse he was going to give." I shrug my shoulders. "Guess he couldn't come up with one."

"Guys suck."

"I think you are right."

It's been nearly two weeks since Tyler stood me up. Almost two weeks since I flirted with some cop who has beautiful blue eyes. I take a bit of my buffalo chicken wrap and hear my phone ding. I wipe my hands and pick up my phone. My notification on my lock screen only shows a random number. Hmm... I swipe to unlock and open the text. My breath nearly catches.

> My asshole friend of a deputy left my card on your car.

How random and yet exciting at the same time. I smile as my fingers slide against the glass.

> Is that so?

Not even a minute later he replies.

> Yes, see I told you I did not leave it on your car.

> Have you been obsessing over this?

> Call it whatever you want, I knew I didn't leave my card and was determined to figure out who left it.

Violet eyes me suspiciously as a giggle leaves my lips. Her face makes this entire thing funnier.

"Remember the cop I told you that I flirted with and completely failed at bringing him back to my bed?"

"Yeah."

"He just texted me. Right now."

Her brown eyes go big. "What did he say?"

"He told me he was not the one who left his business card on my window. He has proof." I laugh.

"That's it? Tell that man to take you on a date." Violet waves a hand at me before she picks up her drink and takes a sip. "Seriously, demand he take you out."

I know I at least have to respond, can't have him thinking he won at whatever game we are playing. Glancing at my phone, I think for a minute about what I should actually say.

Now that we have established it was not you who left the card behind, you can take me out to dinner.

I don't do dates

Never said it was a date, Mr. Grumpy Cop.

Fine

Fine what?

We can grab dinner

Yay!

I have a feeling I am going to regret this.

Then that just means I'll have to make sure I am the greatest regret you will ever have. ;)

· · ·

"Well?" Violet asks impatiently.

"He agreed! He agreed to go out for a bite."

Reality sinks in. Brett just agreed to go out with me. He might not be calling it a date, but I sure am.

* * *

To say I'm nervous would be an understatement. Brett should be here in less than ten minutes. It is so unlike me to be this way. I am very confident in my skin. There's just something about that man though. It could be his intense eyes or that fact that he is a cop and probably did a thorough background check on me. Luckily for the both of us I have no major skeletons in my closet.

Looking at my reflection in the mirror, I tell myself I am beautiful.

I am.

My lips are painted a deep burgundy. Lush red curls fall just past my shoulders. The leopard print headband pairs nicely with the hunter green dress I chose to wear. It is fitted at my chest and flows out before stopping just above my knees. My Jessica Simpson heels match my headband.

A knock sounds at my door, letting me know Brett has arrived. Being the confident woman I am, I take my time answering the door.

And when I finally open the door, holy hell. Standing in front of me is pure perfection.

"Hi," is all I can manage to say because I am too busy checking out the man standing in my doorway.

If I thought Brett looked hot in uniform, shit. Here he stands in a pair of black jeans and a dark plaid button-up. His hair is combed back. He looks sharp. Sexy.

Brett clears his throat, clearly catching me checking him out. "This is not a date."

"Right, not a date." I step past him, catching a whiff of his cologne. It's bold, masculine. A hint of ocean air mixed with a woodsy aroma. He smells way too good for this to not be a date.

We walk in silence to the parking lot of my complex. I stop short when he walks up to a black pickup truck. For some reason I guess I was picturing his police vehicle.

I will say Brett is aiming to please without trying. He stands there and holds the door open for me.

Now I do not consider myself to be a short woman, but I do have to use his running boards to hop up into his truck. So being the lady I am, I slide off my heels and hop right in, making myself at home.

Brett shakes his head and smirks. "I shouldn't expect anything different from you."

"No, you shouldn't. I am who I am." I wink.

Brett goes to shut the door, hesitating just before it closes. He pulls it back a little and looks me in the eye.

"You look beautiful, Finnley."

I sit there in complete shock. Mouth agape and all. His blue eyes never leave mine as he stands there a minute longer. Those gorgeous blue eyes do not leave mine until he finally closes the door. I watch as he shakes his head once before rounding to his side of the truck.

I do not know who he is trying to fool but it is most definitely a date.

Chapter Eight

Brett

I swear this is going to be the longest night of my life. Dinner with the fiery redhead sitting in the passenger seat of my truck is going to damn near kill me. I can already feel it.

It cannot be worse than what Abigail did.

No, nothing can be worse than the shit that woman put me through.

I drive as fast as legally allowed. The quicker I get us to dinner, the quicker I can drop Finnley back off at home. Why the hell did I agree to dinner in the first place? I have been playing it safe since my divorce. No girlfriend, no dating, no one night hookups. Nothing.

So why did I cave? I caved and agreed because the guys, especially Luke, wouldn't get off my ass about taking Finnley out. He asked every single shift. He even went as far as putting my card on her damn car. He knew she would call or text.

He was right.

I do my best to not even glance over at her, but try as I might, she has this allure about her. The dress she has on highlights her red hair perfectly.

She's gorgeous. Fucking gorgeous.

When I pull into the valet parking area, I put my truck in park. Finnley unbuckles and leans down to gather her heels. Her hair falls over her shoulders. She sits back up, heels in hand.

"Are you going to put those back on?"

"Uh, yeah, after I hop out of your big ass truck."

Shaking my head, I smirk. This woman. She is going to test me tonight.

By the time I round my truck, Finnley is already out and sliding on her heels. Leopard print.

She dressed up. I look down at what I am wearing. Nothing special. Jeans and a plaid shirt. I look like shit in comparison with the beauty that stands in front of me with the biggest smile planted on her luscious lips.

"What?" I ask.

"Nothing, Officer. I was just cracking myself up over the fact that you are standing in front of me, taking me out."

I point between us before I start walking. "This is not a date."

"Whatever you say, Officer."

Finnley's words make me stop. I turn fast and face her. My reaction catches her off guard because she dead stops and takes a step back. I probably just scared her.

Shit.

"Finnley, let's get one thing clear. My name is Brett. The only time it is acceptable to call me officer is when you are in trouble with the law, and we want to hope that never happens." I raise an eyebrow, hoping that I haven't scared her too much, but enough to know that I am serious.

Finnley nods while batting those hypnotizing eyes. "So, if I find myself in trouble, doing something illegal, I can call you officer?"

This damn woman. I feel my teeth clench as I turn and walk away.

Chapter Nine

Finnley

After Brett hands his keys over to the valet, we walk the downtown district area. There are so many places to eat here. Which one we are going to? I have no idea. The only thing Brett asked about earlier in the week was if I have any food allergies or a specific type I do not like. That gesture tells me he has to like me even if only slightly.

The second we step into Sage's, the scent of all things Italian hits me. Brett did good. I love me some Italian food.

We follow the hostess to our table. It is tucked away in a corner by a window that has a view of the surrounding nightlife. It's perfect.

"I hope you like Italian food."

"It just so happens that I do." I wink.

Brett looks slightly nervous as nods and takes a sip of his Jack and Coke. I opted for water. There is no way I am drinking tonight. Nope. If I want to get lucky or even make some kind of impression, I need to be sober.

So water it is.

I study the man in front of me while he opens the menu. He's good looking, no, that is not justifiable. He's hot as hell and I would gladly get burned just to have a small slice of Brett Hayworth.

I wonder what he is like in bed? Is his chest covered in tattoos, hair? I have all these questions swirling when the server walks up.

"Do you have any questions about anything on the menu?"

Brett looks at me with one eyebrow raised. I smile and turn my attention to the server. "I do not. I'm ready to order."

The woman, who if I had to guess, is probably in her mid-thirties. Her long blonde hair is braided. She is beautiful. She nods, clicking her pen to let me know she is ready to jot down my order.

"I'll have pappardelle with mushrooms, please."

She nods. "And for you, sir?"

Brett does not look up from his menu. Instead, he keeps his eyes on it and taps his finger on the menu. "I'll have lasagna."

I have to swallow down the laugh that

threatens to escape. No, he did not just order lasagna. Out of everything on this menu, he goes with the safest option.

The server goes on about bringing us our side salads and some bread. I just shake my head, not really listening. As soon as she walks out of earshot, I laugh. Finally.

"What's so funny?" Brett asks, clearly confused. It makes me laugh harder.

As soon as my laughter subsides, I shake my head. "Brett, I must know, do you always go with the safest meal on the menu?"

"What is wrong with lasagna? It's a classic dish."

I laugh again. "Nothing is wrong with it. It is just, there were many delicious options on that menu. You could have picked anything else. I mean I can cook lasagna at home. But pappardelle, no way, I would never attempt."

He shakes his head. "You're crazy. You know that, right?"

I shrug my shoulder, allowing my hair to fall over it. I lean down and take a sip of my water. "I'm aware that I'm too much for some people. I never claim to be someone I am not."

"Fair enough."

"Now that we have that out of the way. Tell me something about you, Brett."

"I don't date."

"I am aware. You did say this was not a date." I wink. "If I remember correctly, you mentioned no longer being married. I'm guessing she divorced you because of your career."

I throw him a confident look. I took a course in college. Police officers and first responders have a high divorce rate. Their careers are demanding, and some woman cannot handle being put on the back burner.

Brett presses his lips together and picks up his drink. He brings it to his lips but does not take a sip.

"Tell me I'm wrong."

"You are wrong," he deadpans before finally taking a drink.

"I can't be that far off."

"Way off."

"Okay, so tell me, why are you no longer married?"

"Are you always so nosey?" he asks before taking another swallow.

"Are you always so grumpy?"

Brett sets the glass down, and I watch the amber liquid dance around the cubes of ice.

He is hiding something. Has to be. He's way too closed off. Of course, it could be that his career made him this way. I decide to change the subject.

"Your turn, ask me anything."

"Do you usually allow strangers to take you to dinner?"

"If they are hot enough." I wink which causes him to shake his head.

"You really shouldn't go out with people you don't know." His voice is stern. It almost makes me laugh.

"You know, Brett, you really need to take a chill pill. I bet you could be a lot more fun if you let loose."

He shakes his head and opens his mouth to say something but stops as our server walks up with a tray holding our dinners.

I hope he holds that thought.

Unfortunately for me, he is quiet once she walks away.

Whatever he was about to say is forever lost.

* * *

"Would you like to walk around some before I bring you home?" Brett asks as we walk out of Sage's.

I glance at my phone. It is early still. "Let's walk. The night is still young. There is still trouble to find."

"Finnley," Brett warns.

I nudge him with my elbow. "Loosen up."

"In most cases, trouble gets people in trouble with the law. If you haven't noticed by now, I am the law, so I tend to steer clear of problematic situations."

"That's fair. But a little fun never hurt anyone."

"My wife cheated on me."

Wow, that came out of left field. So wasn't expecting that.

"That sucks." What else do I say? Sorry? No, because I am not the one who cheated. I do not owe him that apology.

Blue eyes look down at me. He's a good foot or so taller than me. Brett's eyes do the talking. He is nervous. He hasn't done something like this in a while.

I nod as if I get it. I mean I was stood up recently, have been dumped, and left heartbroken. So yeah, this whole dating thing makes us vulnerable. It does suck in a way.

Without thinking, I reach my hand out for his. He immediately freezes at my touch and his steps come to a halt, yet he does not pull away.

"Finnley, what are you doing?" Brett looks down between us where our hands are now joined.

I shrug. "Just going for a walk with you." I start to walk and tug at his hand to get him to follow. He hesitates for a second before finally putting one foot in front of the other.

You can do this, Brett.

"This is not a date."

"So, you've said."

The rest of our stroll through the downtown district is quiet. No words are said.

We don't need words. We just need each other.

Chapter Ten

Finnley

"This actually tastes good." Brett's words come after he takes the spoon of raspberry truffle ice cream out of his mouth.

"See! And to think, you were going to go with boring chocolate chip."

"Yeah, yeah."

"Hey, sometimes it's fun to try new things. Do something spontaneous."

Brett shakes his head while continuing to eat his ice cream. I went with mocha almond in a waffle cone.

"There is more to life than boring Brett."

"I am not boring. I live a simple life."

I think about his words for a minute. His wife cheated and now he is probably a homebody who just exists. Nothing more.

"Do you ever get sick of simple?"

"No," he clips fast.

Clearly it is a sensitive subject. I decide it's best to drop it. I don't want to ruin our evening because despite him being slightly grumpy. I've enjoyed being in his presence. It's different than other guys I've gone out with. I can't quite explain it.

I take my last bite, and a shiver runs through me.

"Cold?"

"I wasn't until just now."

Brett nods as he throws his cup in the trash. He steps a little closer to me yet doesn't dare make contact.

"It is a little chilly out. I suppose we should get going."

I nod, almost sad that our time together is almost up. Will he want to go out again? There is no telling. He gives nothing away.

When his truck is brought around, I slide out of my heels once more. He is polite, opening the door for me. I step on the runner and turn to lean into Brett's ear. I feel him freeze and it makes me giggle.

"Relax, Brett. I was just going to say thank you for opening the door."

He lets out a breath and eyes me with those piercing blues. "You're welcome, Finnley. Get in so I can take you home."

I can't be positive, but I swear I saw a slight

smirk when he told me to get in. Maybe, just maybe I am breaking down the walls the surround him.

When we pull into my complex, a sense of familiarity hits me. I do not have to give him my gate code. He already knows it. There is also the unfamiliar feeling of not being drunk. I am sober, unlike last time. I hope that works in my favor at least some. Otherwise, I may feel like a fool.

As soon as Brett puts his truck in park, he hops out. Almost in a rush. Sadness seeps in. He cannot wait to get rid of me.

I am unable to read his face when he opens my door. The man is stone cold.

I hop down. "Thank you."

"You're welcome, Finnley."

I try hard not to focus on the chill that runs down my spine due to the way he said my name. I don't want to get my hopes up.

Nope. Not going there.

By the time we reach my door, I am a ball of nerves. Up until the drive home I had a clear picture of how I wanted this moment to go, but now... Now all thoughts are jumbled. I look up at Brett, hoping he will take the lead.

He looks just as lost as me.

Fuck, Finnley. Get your act together. One of you needs to be in control.

I put on a smile. "I had a nice time with you

tonight." I pause, I want to say more yet don't want to scare him off.

"Surprisingly I had a nice time as well. It wasn't as painful as I expected it to be." A playful smile pulls at his lips--just barely, yet I see it.

I grab my chest dramatically. "I'm offended. I am a blast to be around."

"Says you."

"Ugh, double offended!" I say as take my keys out of my purse. Now is the time to speak up. "Can I invite you in?"

I watch as confusion crosses his features. He was not expecting my offer.

He opens his mouth to speak but nothing comes out. He finally clears his throat. "We hardly know one another."

"So, I'm a cool person. You're grumpy. It will make for a great time."

"I am not grumpy. I am simple, like I said."

"Grumpy, simple, whatever. So, what do you say?" I reach out and squeeze his upper arm. All muscle.

His eyes fly to where my hand is touching him. There is a tic and I can't be certain, but I think I see a war wagering in his eyes as he takes a step back. My hand falls back to my side. Maybe he doesn't like to be touched. Or maybe he isn't used to it. There is no telling.

After a few moments of awkward silence, he speaks.

"I think it is best that I go."

As much as I don't want to admit it, his words crush my spirit. They shouldn't. Like he said, we hardly know each other. I open my door and step halfway in before turning to face him.

"Okay, well, tonight was nice. Thank you."

Brett nods and takes a step toward me. "I might regret asking, but would you like to grab dinner again sometime?"

I smile. "Only if it is date next time."

He shakes his head. "Fine."

You know what, fuck it. Letting go of the door, I walk up to Brett and lean in to place a kiss on his lips. He turns fast at the last minute and my lips land on his cheek instead.

"Finnley. This was not a date."

"Who says we have to follow the rules?"

"Me. I follow the rules." He pauses. "And Finnley." Brett stops. "Lock your door."

I roll my eyes and close the door, locking it. Of course I will lock my door. I'm no dummy.

I kick off my heels and plop down on my couch. I replay the last five minutes over and over.

Brett asked to take me out again. A date. He wouldn't let me kiss him because this was not a date. Does that mean the next time I make a move to kiss him, he'll allow it because it will be a date? If so, I am okay with that.

If I learned anything about that gorgeous man tonight, it's that Brett seems to like to play by the rules.

Chapter Eleven

Brett

I cannot believe I asked Finnley out again.

I agreed to a date.

What the hell is wrong with me?

"Yo, Hayworth, what's with you? She getting to you already?" Luke throws a fry at me.

"Watch it," I say while wiping the greasy salt from my uniform. We are both on shift and decided to hit a fast-food joint for lunch. I already regret it.

I should've known better than to come to him. Huge fucking mistake. Luke may be my friend, hell I even consider him family. However, I should've known better than to tell him I was taking Finnley out for a second time.

"Well?"

"No, she is not getting to me. I'm not sure why I asked her out again."

"You gonna get laid this time?" he asks while shoving a fry in his mouth.

I just ignore him and take a bite of my sandwich.

"Not gonna lie, she is a hot little red head. Cute ass."

"Do not talk about Finnley like that. Ever. Again." My words are clipped with anger.

Luke laughs and shakes his head. If I didn't execute all control, I would have reached across the table and decked him. Why does he always have to rile me up?

Because he knows.

He knows that my wife did a number on me and that I haven't been with a single woman since her. They aren't worth the trouble.

"Okay, humor me then, why did you bother to ask her out again?"

Fucker doesn't know when to stop.

"I don't know. She kept things light. I didn't feel like I was pressured to please her."

"Ha. We all know you will fail at the pleasing part. It's been how long?" He laughs again.

"Doesn't matter how long it has been."

"Sure, it does."

"Finnley came on to me, now fuck off." I hate that I told him something personal about her, however, I knew he would not let up until I gave him something.

"Oh real—" He stops short when we hear the sound of our radios.

Lunch time is over.

* * *

Why the hell am I so nervous? I've been pacing the house for the past forty-five minutes. Because it's Saturday evening and that means it's almost time to leave to pick up Finnley for dinner.

She texted me earlier in the week asking if we could go to the Iron Rose Pub since that is where we first met. I agreed even though I had another place in mind, somewhere nicer. It's not that the pub isn't nice, I just wanted to make a good impression.

Fuck.

Why do I need to make a good impression?

I pass the mirror in the hallway, knowing I don't need to check myself. I did that a few times already. Dressed in a black polo and denim jeans. Can't really fuck that up. Shaking my head, I check my watch. It's time.

I grab my keys, and for the first time in a very long time, uncertainty fills my mind.

I knock once, taking a step back. I hear the lock and then she appears.

There is no denying that Finnley is beautiful, but hell if she does not look hot as fuck.

Standing before me, she is dressed in a very tight, ivory low-cut top. It tucks into her black slacks while still showing off all her curves. She skipped the heels tonight. Instead, she went with a pair of sandals. Her hair is down, fanned around her face.

Simple, yet hot.

Finnley clears her throat. "Like what you see?"

Shit.

I smile and shake my head. "You look beautiful."

"Thanks. You know you don't look so bad your-self. Especially when you smile." She pats my chest.

"Come on, lock your door."

"Yes, Officer."

"Finnley," I warn.

She laughs. "Yeah, yeah, I'm not to call you that unless I am in trouble."

This woman is testing me already and we haven't even made it to dinner. Something tells me it's going to be a long night.

I've just pulled out of her apartment complex when she leans over to me, sniffing. It almost weirds me out.

"You know, Brett, you smell sexy."

"What?" I can't help but ask.

"You smell sexy. Like you smell good. It is a compliment."

"Oh."

I am not sure what else to say. Luke was right. I have no idea what I'm doing, like a fish out of water.

It doesn't take us long to get to the Iron Rose. Once in, Finnley seems to take charge and walks right up to the hostess stand. I stand back and watch her do her thing for a minute. She is confident in her skin. I'm not sure how no other guy has scooped her up.

"Come on, Brett." Finnley tosses her hair back as she glances at me. I follow her and the hostess to a booth near the bar. Three TVs are hung in the area, each one different baseball games.

"I figured you might want to see some of the game," Finnley says casually while reaching for the menu.

"What makes you think I watch baseball?"

"I don't know. You are single, and most men watch some type of sports."

Well, she got me there.

"See?" She smiles big.

Shaking my head, I study the menu. I need a distraction. The pub has a Saturday night special on wings. Maybe I'll do that.

"Want to share some wings?"

My head shoots up quickly, and it must startle her because she sits back and eyes me.

"You read my mind. I was just thinking about ordering wings."

She claps. "Oh good! Want all one flavor or should we do two?"

"Two."

"Yay! I'll pick one and you pick one."

"Deal," I reply while wondering if this is a dream or reality. I cannot recall a time I ever shared wings with my ex-wife.

A few minutes go by in silence before Finnley speaks up.

"Okay, now don't laugh. I choose garlic parmesan."

"What?" I nearly laugh. "That's not a wing flavor."

"Sure it is. It says so right here." Her nails that are painted a dark shade of red point to the menu.

"Fine. I am going with hot."

Once our orders are in, Finnley excuses herself to the restroom. I decide to focus on the game that is on TV until I hear her phone ding. I glance at it for a split second and then direct my attention back to the screen. Not even thirty seconds later, her phone goes off again. This time when I look at it, I catch a notification from an app I have not heard of. Curiosity gets the best of me, and I look up the name.

To my surprise, it's a dating app. What is someone as beautiful as her doing on a dating site and why is she getting notifications while out with me?

I try not to dwell on it. Not that I have a right to question or know. Maybe she has not been on the site in a while and someone decided to swipe left or whatever it is they do.

When Finnley returns, she picks up her phone and scrunches her face and shakes her head before putting her away.

"Everything okay?"

"Yes, couldn't be better."

I am not sure why, but her words bring me relief. While I know that this is a date, I don't see us going much further. I have no desire for any sort of relationship. If I really think about it, I am cruel for even being out with the gorgeous woman seated across from me. I feel bad for possibly getting her hopes up, however, I know it's better this way.

Safer.

As soon as our wings are brought out, Finnley wastes no time digging in. She grabs one of each and I watch as she pours some ranch dressing on her plate. She's so carefree. So sure of herself and while I struggle to admit it, I like that about her.

When she is done, she looks at me. "Are you going to try one of the garlic parm ones?" she asks before popping her finger into her mouth. The way she does it makes my cock twitch. Where did the come from? It takes me a few to register my cock straining.

What the hell?

I need to refocus on something else. Anything else.

"Yeah, I'll try one even though it has no heat to it."

Finnley huffs at my remark as if she is offended. She isn't though, I can tell by the smile that is plastered on her face.

"Okay, Mister, I like hot things. Sometimes change tastes good." Giving me a wink, she goes back to eating.

"I like what I like. Nothing wrong with that."

"No, nothing is wrong with that. I'm just saying, sometimes it's fun to try something new."

Shaking my head, I grab a garlic whatever it is called and take a bite. Finnley looks at me with amusement dancing in her eyes. Surprisingly it tastes good. I won't tell her that though.

"Tried something new. Happy now?"

"And? Did you like it?"

"It was all right."

Finnley claps her hands together. "You did like it. It was written all over your face!"

She sits back and takes a sip of her drink. Why do I allow this woman to get under my skin? *Because your dumb ass asked her out again.*

"You know, Brett, there is so much more to life

than just existing. You should give it a try. Don't just breathe, live."

I think about her words for a moment while chewing up another hot wing. "Don't just breathe, live." That would make me vulnerable, and I promised myself I would never be vulnerable again.

"Let me ask you something, Finnley."

"Ask away."

"Have you ever been hurt by someone?"

She hesitates. "Well, yeah."

"I was hurt in the worst way. I choose to live this way so no one can ever have that power again. No one can hurt me if I don't give them the power to."

Finnley bites off a piece of celery and nods her head. I can tell she is processing everything I just said to her. Gone is the smile that was upon her face. Maybe now she sees where I'm coming from.

"I can understand that to a point. I really can. I was stood up the night I met you. It hurt, and the fact that he showed his face before deciding to bail hurt more. That means he saw me and that I was not good enough for him." She waves a hand over her face before sighing. "But Brett, if I really let that hurt consume me, I wouldn't be here with you tonight." She smiles but it's a sad smile.

I nod. She has a point. A point I'm unsure about. What if?

Chapter Twelve

Finnley

Brett's been hurt. That much is clear. I know he said his ex-wife cheated. I have no details and given how closed off he is, I do not think prying will help.

What I do know is that Brett needs a new outlook on life. He needs to see that not all is bad. I can be the one to show him, that is if he will allow it.

"Enough with the heavy. Tell me something else about you," I say as soon as the server walks away from dropping the check on our table.

Brett doesn't reach for it, instead he grabs reaches into his back pocket and pulls out a black leather wallet.

"There's not much to know. I'm a boring person," he says while pulling out a card and setting it on top of the bill.

He has to give me more than that. I stare at him with a raised eyebrow. As soon as he realizes that I want more of a response, he sighs.

"Fine. My favorite color is blue."

"My favorite color is a deep red."

"Like the color of your lips?"

I'm taken aback. I was not expecting that from Mr. Grumpy Cop. The fact that he pays attention to my lips gives me chills. Especially since my lips are bare tonight. I wore a deep red on our "not a date" dinner.

"Yes. I must say I am a little impressed that you paid attention to the color of my lips."

There is a tic in Brett's jaw. I find the movement hot as hell. His strong jaw line flexes as he goes to speak.

"I did notice. I notice everything, Finnley."

Unsure of what to say, I just nod. If I didn't have chills before, I certainly have them now.

Brett is quiet as we walk to his truck. A part of me wants to speak up, make a move. Something, except I fear chasing him off. Brett may be closed off, yet for some reason, I enjoy being around him.

When we reach the truck, Brett holds the door open for me. I hop up on the running board and turn toward him.

"Thank you for dinner, Brett." And before he can say anything, I lean down and kiss his cheek. I don't wait for a reaction. Instead, I climb in and put my seatbelt on. Brett, on the other hand, stands there frozen and completely in shock as he stares at me. I can't help but laugh.

"Relax, I only kissed your cheek. Imagine if I had kissed your lips..."

"Finnley," he interrupts while shaking his head.

It makes me laugh more. Maybe I'm breaking down the walls that he hides behind, or I've embarrassed him. Either way, this girl is not giving up any time soon.

The entire drive home he lets me control the radio. He acts annoyed, but deep down I think he secretly likes my out-of-tune singing.

Once his truck is in park, Brett reaches for the knob and turns down the music. He does not make eye contact with me. No, he stares out the windshield and into the darkness.

I decide I need to be the one to break the silence. Brett never will. He doesn't know how to.

"Come on, walk me to my door."

Of course I am going to invite him in. He just doesn't need to know that yet.

Baby steps.

Looking at Brett, it's obvious that he's uncomfortable. It takes me a split second to make up my mind on what to do. I unlock my door and casually walk in, leaving it open so that Brett has no option but to follow.

Or at least I hope he does.

I do not look back as I reach the kitchen. Relief floods me when I hear the front door shut and lock. I let out a breath I didn't know I was holding. He didn't turn and run. That has to mean something, right?

I cast a look over my shoulder as I open the fridge. "Can I get you a drink?"

"I'm good."

"Okay, if you change your mind, help yourself."

"Uh, thanks."

Pulling out the Malibu, I smile as reality sets in that he didn't just turn and leave. He could have said goodnight from the doorway. He didn't though. That's good, I think. I'm hoping it'll help him slowly come out of his shell.

When I come out of the kitchen with my drink, I find Brett standing in my small living room. My couch is small, fake, gray leather. There is a throw blanket that my grandmother made from my old running shirts laid out across the back of it. Against the wall are three bookshelves, filled with books. So many books. A few canvas paintings hang on the wall. Each one, I hand painted. A variety of land-scapes in a multitude of colors.

Brett spins in slow circle before stopping in front of me.

"No TV?"

I smile and shake my head. "Nope. No TV."

Brett looks like he might go into shock at my words. I can't help but chuckle. "Don't look so surprised. Not everyone you meet watches TV." I point to my bookshelf. "Books, reading, is my jam."

"I can see that," he replies while rubbing his chin.

Walking over to my couch, I plop down. "Come join me." I pat the spot next to me.

Brett walks over, and I can tell he is debating his next move. He is fighting a silent war in his head. It makes me sad for him, and I want to say something but refrain. He needs to do this on his own.

When he finally sits down, I turn to him and smile. He smiles back.

"You are different, Finnley."

"I know."

And I do. I am different. I own it. I am me.

I just hope it will be enough for the man sitting next to me.

Chapter Thirteen

Brett

What the hell am I doing in Finnley's apartment? Sitting on her couch no less. It's a recipe for disaster. I can practically taste it. Yet, I make no move to leave.

Finnley takes a sip of what I can only assume is something mixed with Malibu because I can smell the coconut.

"What are you drinking?"

"They call it a Tokyo Sunset. I tried it once at the Disney Vero Beach Resort while I was on vacation a few years ago. I've been hooked since."

I nod at her response.

"Want to try it?" Finnley holds the drink out in front of me.

"I'm good."

"Oh, come on. I don't have cooties, Brett. A little sip won't hurt you."

Sighing, I give in. "Fine."

As I take the tumbler from her, her pale hands brush against mine. I feel something like a shock and look at her. Huge mistake because it's clear by the look on her face that she felt it too. Her perfect lips are parted as if she wants to speak but she is stunned into silence.

Fuck.

This cannot happen. I take a quick chug in an effort to focus on something else. Something other than her lips.

Anything other than her lips.

I try hard to focus on the taste as it hits my tongue. It's sweet. I get hints of coconut rum and banana at first, but then I taste the pineapple. It's good. Very sweet but good. I still prefer whiskey.

"Well, do you like it?" Finley asks. Her hazel eyes sparkle in anticipation.

"It's a girly drink, too sweet."

She gives me a little shove. "Oh hush. It is good though. I saw it on your face. Admit it."

"It was all right."

No way in hell will I ever tell her that I thought it was good or that the look on my face was probably due to my thoughts about her lips.

My cock twitches for the second time tonight. Now is not the time for that shit. I need to get out of here.

Handing Finnley back her sweet drink, I sigh. I am so out of touch here. It's been years since I've gone on a date. Abigail was the first and last woman I dated. I don't know what to even say or where to go from here. I just know that I need to leave and fast.

Finnley takes a sip of her drink. "Don't do that. Don't get all grumpy on me."

"What?"

"You went some place. I saw it on your face. Wherever you went, it doesn't make you happy, so don't go there."

"I... I didn't go anywhere." Hell, now the woman can read me like an open book. How does she do it? I rub my chin while debating my next move and how to get out of this apartment.

"You did. I saw it. Don't go there. Stay here with me. I had a nice time tonight, Brett. I'd like to think you did too."

"It has been quite a while since I've gone on a date."

"Nonsense. We went out last week."

"That was not a—"

She cuts me off before I can finish. "A date, right. It didn't count. But tonight counts. That must mean something."

"Finnley, I had a nice time. But I don't think I can—"

My words are cut off for the second time tonight as her lips land on mine. I can taste the rum on her lips. I freeze, unsure of what to do at first. I'm like a damn fish out of water.

Thankfully my cock and brain seem to be communicating because as soon as I feel her tongue, my mouth parts, allowing her to deepen our kiss. I instantly taste the rum. I won't lie. She tastes good.

It doesn't take long before Finnley leans into me. I feel her hands land on my shoulders, making their way around my neck. I should stop this and pull away yet, I cannot seem to make myself do it. Feeling my cock harden is a sure sign that trouble lurks ahead.

It is as if I have zero control over my body right now. The panic grows along with my cock. I'm almost certain she can feel it too.

Kind of hard not to.

I reach up, taking a fistful of her hair, hoping to still her. It causes her to pull back. It worked, I think, until she smiles against my lips.

"I like it rough," she says before descending on me once more.

Instantly, my hand falls from her hair. If my cock wasn't hard before, it sure as hell is now. What the hell?

I need to put a stop to this right now.

I don't though. I allow her to continue kissing me.

I should not be enjoying the way she kisses me. I should not like the way she tastes.

My mind is at war with itself. My hands are frozen at my sides. They are itching to touch her, and I refuse. I fear what will happen if I do. I fear I will want to touch every part of her. That I will want more than just kissing and that is way to fucking dangerous.

I don't want things. I don't need things. I sure as hell don't need to be kissing this gorgeous woman, so why am here doing stupid shit?

When Finnley finally pulls back an inch to catch her breath, she leans her head against mine. It is then that I feel it. How both our hearts are pounding, and we are out of breath. Desire lingers in the air.

"Finnley," I say through gritted teeth.

"Shh, don't ruin this. Whatever it is. Don't ruin it, just feel it. Feel it with me for a moment."

I sit there with her, not saying a single word. I decide I can do that. No words. No talking. That seems easy enough, right?

Ha.

My brain is running a thousand miles a second it seems. It is replaying everything. Her lips. The way she tasted like rum. The way she touched me. I replay all of it.

The worst part... I actually enjoyed it.
Fuck.
This is bad.
So damn bad.

Chapter Fourteen

Finnley

ow.

That is all I got.

No words.

I am not sure what came over me. Whatever it was, I'm glad I made the move because Brett's lips on mine was a delicious experience.

We sit here in silence as we both catch our breath. I can't help but wonder what Brett was going to say before I cut him off with my lips. My brain is foggy, but I think he was about to tell me he didn't think he could do this. As in us dating.

I sit up straight. "We just kissed. No big deal,

okay. Let's not make a big deal out of what just happened."

Brett hesitates mid-nod. "Yeah, okay. No big deal."

I force a smile. "Just live in the moment. Life is easier that way."

"Easier said than done," he replies as he stands, straightening his shirt.

He looks over his shoulder toward my door. I can sense his next move. He is leaving.

"I should get going."

Called it. Brett is practically an open book. I can read him so well. He will not meet my eyes. In fact, he looks anywhere except at me. He's uncomfortable and unsure. The tension is growing between us, threatening to choke what is left of the night.

"Okay. Let me walk you to the door," I say as I set my drink down and stand. The butterflies I felt minutes before begin to slowly fade away.

It takes mere seconds to reach my door since my apartment isn't that big. As soon as I unlock and open the door, he steps through as if being on the other side of the threshold will keep him safe.

"I had a nice time, Brett. Maybe we can do this again and you don't have to call it a date." I wink, hoping to lighten the mood that has suddenly gone south.

"Yeah, maybe."

"So that's not a no?"

"Also not a yes."

His face gives nothing away so I cannot tell if he is being funny or serious. Given what I do know, I should just assume he is serious.

"Okay then." I shrug while trying to play it cool.

Brett nods and walks to the stairwell. As soon as his boots hit the first step, I turn to shut the door but stop short when he calls my name.

When I look back at him, I see it. The war is evident in his ocean blues. It is written all over his face.

It gives me hope. Hope can be tricky though. I tell myself not to read into it.

"Yeah?"

"The last woman I kissed was my wife."

Holy shit. Talk about dropping a truth bomb. How long has he been divorced? Did he tell me? I can't recall. I won't be asking either. At least not tonight. How do I even respond to that? I don't know.

"Then I am honored that you let me be the one after her." I smile and hope like hell that it eases whatever fight he is mentally fighting right now. I really do because I want there to be another date, another kiss. He might think he's broken, but I don't. He just needs to be shown that he is whole and worthy of love.

I like Brett.

He's different even when he's grumpy.

That's why I like him.

* * *

"No, Violet, I am not exactly holding out for Brett. I am just seeing where we go."

Violet's voice comes through the speakers as I drive south to meet a new doctor that just opened a practice. "Whatever, at least answer Tyler back. Maybe let him make it up to you."

"You think I should? Even after he stood me up?"

"Give him a chance to explain. Maybe he got nervous seeing a hot chick."

I laugh. "You got the hot part right. I guess texting him won't hurt. I'll give him one more shot and then that is it."

"Sounds fair."

I sigh into the phone as I pull into a parking lot. "Listen, I just got to my next client. Chat later?"

"You know it."

"Loves, bye," I say as I hang up and get out of Onyx.

Popping open the trunk, I start gathering what I need. I pause to shoot Tyler a quick text.

Maybe giving Tyler a second chance won't be

such a bad idea and even though I really like Brett, he is closed off.

I'd be keeping my options open.

A sudden tinge a guilt runs through my bones. I should not feel any guilt though. It's not like Brett and I are exclusive. Hell, we are not anything. Just two people who went to dinner. A guy I kissed.

No big deal.

* * *

"Weekend starts now," I say as I close my laptop. It's after five on a Friday. I have no plans to open it again until Monday. Right now, the only thing on my mind is my date with Tyler.

At first, I was leery about giving him another shot. However, we've been talking all week and I have a good feeling about our date. I told him we could go anywhere but the Iron Rose. I feel like it would be bad juju or something.

I put my laptop on charge and head for the bathroom to get ready. I had taken a shower earlier, so I just need to get dressed and do my makeup.

I slip into an olive mini dress that I will pair with a pair of tan wedges. Staring at myself in the mirror, I am still unsure of what to do with my wild red hair. Do I curl it or throw it in a braid?

Unable to make up my mind, I make a move to start my makeup. I go with a simple and classy look. A mixture of nudes and gold that make my hazel eyes pop. Nude lips. I finish with mascara.

Once finished, I check my phone. I need to leave soon. Tyler did offer to come pick me up, but I declined. I'm not comfortable enough to allow some stranger to just pick me up at my apartment. Brett would be proud, I tell myself.

Speaking of that man. His name flashes across my screen. It kind of surprises me. Brett has been distant this week. A few short texts here and there. I will not fault him for it though. I haven't put much effort into talking to him. I've been too caught up in Tyler.

Swiping, I open his text.

What are you doing tonight?

Guilt threatens to choke me while I bite my lip nervously and debate how to reply to that. It's such a simple question, yet a hard one. I remind myself that I'm not doing anything wrong. I type and untype my reply several times before finally settling on one.

> I am going out for the evening. Do you have anything going on this weekend?

Satisfied with my response, I slide my phone into my purse and grab my car keys. I am into Brett and really like being around him, it is just that he is far from wanting any type of commitment. I won't fault him for it but will also not be waiting at home. Like Violet said, I need to keep my options open.

I arrive at dinner a few minutes late thanks to rush hour traffic on a Friday night. Secretly, I hope it causes Tyler to squirm in his seat. Maybe, if I'm lucky, it will make him worry the way I worried a few weeks ago.

I walk into the Pink Elephant and up to the hostess stand. The feeling of excitement courses through me. Tonight will be fun. I am sure of it. The Pink Elephant is a local hot spot. It's a little cafe known for playing great live music and good food.

Grabbing my braid that I went with last minute, I start twirling the ends and I tell the woman standing there that I am meeting someone.

She looks at me and smiles brightly. "Oh yes, right this way. The gentleman said he was expecting a beautiful woman with red hair. He wasn't lying." She pushes her blonde bangs out of her face and waves for me to follow. "Come on."

I smile and follow her while silently gushing over her words. Tyler told a stranger I was beautiful.

We round a corner, and I spot him right away. He is looking down at his phone, sitting in a small booth. Even from a distance, I can tell he looks good. His light brown hair is shaggy, covers his forehead. It doesn't touch his shoulders, though it is close.

The hostess sets my menu down across from Tyler. It causes him to pop his head up instantly. His blue eyes light up as he smiles big. He stands up to greet me, grabbing my hands.

"Finnley, it is great to finally meet you." He shakes his head and laughs. "Wow, that came out really lame."

I smile and laugh a little myself. "Yeah." I can already tell it is going to be good night. "Shall we?" I say as I nod to the booth.

"Oh yeah." He gestures for me to have a seat, and I do.

I can't help but look at him. Talking to someone and sending pictures via a dating app can be sketchy, like you never know if someone is trying to catfish you. Tyler was honest there.

"I was a little worried you were coming for

payback and planned on not showing," he admits as he runs a hand through his hair.

"Really?"

Good. I secretly like that he was stressing. He deserved to sweat some.

"Yeah, I mean I was a dick for standing you up and avoiding you."

"Yeah, well you're here now. Let's start fresh."

Tyler nods and looks down at the menu. "I've never been here. What's good?"

"Anything. I haven't had a bad meal yet."

And I mean it. I haven't. The Pink Elephant has some delicious sandwiches and wraps. I already know what I'm ordering. That is how confident I am in their food.

"I'm getting a buffalo bacon and ranch chicken wrap."

Tyler looks up at me. "That sounds good. I think I'll do the same."

"You will not be disappointed."

As soon as our server takes our order, I ask the question that has been on the tip on my tongue since I spotted him.

"Okay, now that I am here and did not stand you up, tell me what happened. Why did you show and leave?"

Tyler grimaces. Good, he should feel horrible. It has been the one question that I have allowed him to avoid. Until tonight that is.

"I, uh, I saw someone that I am not on good terms with. It freaked me out and I took off."

I squint my eyes, confused at his response. It was not at all what I was expecting. The look on my face must say the same because Tyler shakes his head.

"I'm serious. I know it sounds like a shit story. You have to believe me though. I did a shitty thing years ago, and that person has never forgiven me. I didn't want to be on a date with you and then have them spot me. They would have made a scene. I couldn't do it. So, I chickened out and took off."

I guess that can make sense. I nod in understanding. "Okay, I believe you and just this once I will forgive you."

"Thank you. I'm really sorry about what I did to you. You have no idea." He sighs.

I feel my phone vibrate and reach into my purse. Three texts from Brett. I'll respond later. Right now, I am with someone.

Sliding my phone back away, I smile. Time to get to know Tyler a little better.

Chapter Fifteen

Finnley

"I had a nice time," I say as I stand from the booth. I honestly did. Our conversation flowed the entire time.

Tyler takes the last sip of his beer before standing. "Me too. I am really glad you didn't stand me up."

"You are lucky." I laugh.

He grabs the back of his neck. "Yeah, I am."

At least he knows it.

When I start walking toward the exit, I feel my phone vibrate in my bag. There's no way Brett is still texting me. I reach in and sure enough now there are five texts from him and one from Violet. Three missed calls.

All from Brett.

I feel my face growing red. He must want to get a hold of me. That thought alone gives me chills.

But right now, I am with Tyler.

I slide my phone back into my purse and tell myself I'll respond as soon as I get in Onyx.

"So, can I see you again?" Tyler asks as soon as we step outside onto the sidewalk.

I try to swallow all thoughts of Brett before turning to face Tyler.

"Woah, you okay? Your face is beet red."

So much for hiding it.

"Yeah, I get flushed easily. Fair skin and all that." My hand circles my face. I hope he buys my bullshit. That really isn't bullshit, it happens.

"Oh, okay."

Tyler looks everywhere but at me, and I instantly feel like shit. He might have stood me up, but he made up for that tonight.

"I like that idea."

"What?" he asks.

"You wanted to see me again. I think I would like that."

"Really?" His face lights up.

"Yeah. Text me, okay?"

Tyler nods as I begin walking away. I think he's in shock that I agreed for a second date. I mean why not? He gave me an explanation. One that I totally get. I have my own family drama. Drama that I stay far away from. I moved an hour away just to avoid the daily crap. Who knew that one hour would make all the difference.

My sister Fia carries enough baggage for a baseball team and not the good kind of baggage either. She is a shit-stirrer and thrives on gossip.

Thankfully she is five years older than I am, so we never ran in the same circles. However, she always brought the tea home, and I could not wait to get away so I could have a peaceful cup of coffee.

As soon as I get into my car, I pull my phone back out and open my text from Violet first.

I want to know everything. Call me as soon as your date is over.

I laugh and move on, opening Brett's texts. Two are sent back to back. I check the time stamp, they were sent just after I responded to him.

No plans. Just watching the game at home

You must think I am boring

The next few texts come about forty minutes later.

Are you going out alone?

Finnley, are you okay?

I know you said you were heading out, I just want to make sure you are good.

There is no way Brett is worried about me. He is too closed off to care about anyone except maybe himself.

But... he did drive my drunk ass home. He must care to some point.

Right?

I should text him and at least let him know I am not lying dead in some alley.

I'm good. Heading home.

As soon as I hit send, a shadow appears in my driver mirror. My hand moves fast to lock the door. At the same time, the shadow knocks on my window. I let out a shriek before hearing a voice.

"Relax, it's just me, Tyler. It is okay." Tyler puts his hands up in surrender.

What the fuck? Tyler?

I look and see that it is him. This isn't odd at all. I sigh, in an attempt to get my heart to calm down.

Putting the window down a little, I finally speak. "You scared me."

"Sorry, I didn't mean to. I just, um... I wanted to make sure you got to your car okay. I felt like a loser for not walking you to your car."

"Oh, that is nice of you. I'm good though."

"Okay, I just wanted to make sure. I didn't mean to scare you."

"It's okay, Tyler."

He waves and disappears back into the darkness. I waste no time putting my window back up and hitting the lock button again just for good measure.

I try to tell myself that Tyler was just being kind, yet part of me is screaming that what he did was slightly creepy. What guy follows a woman at a distance to their car? That part is overtaking the kind gesture. Up until this point, he gave me no strange vibes.

My phone starts ringing through the speakers of my car, causing me to jump for a second time in less than five minutes.

"Shit!" I shout as I reach forward in a rush to answer the call without bothering to see who it is.

"Hello!"

"Finnley? Are you okay? You don't sound okay."

The sound of Brett's deep voice coming through my speakers calms me. Almost instantly, my heart rate begins to settle. Hearing his voice is kind of soothing. I should find that odd, yet I don't.

"Finnley, are you still there? Talk to me."

Shit, I never responded to him, too caught up in my head.

"Shit. Sorry. I'm good."

"Yeah? You sure? Because you don't sound good."

Putting my car in reverse, I continue chatting. "Yes, I was just out, and my friend startled me. I thought they left, but um... they forgot something and scared me at my car."

"Oh."

I can tell by the sound of his voice that he is not buying it. Even though it's the truth, my words don't seem sure. A wild thought pops in my head.

"Would you like me to stop by on my way home? Let you see for yourself."

Brett is quiet. So quiet that I glance at my touch screen to make sure the call is still up. Now it's my turn to ask questions.

"Brett?"

"That won't be necessary. I was just concerned because you were not responding."

"Were you worried about me?"

"Finnley," his voice warns.

"What? I only asked a question."

"Did you have a nice time out with your friend?"

"I did." Saying it out loud, however, makes me feel slightly crummy. I know I have told myself several times tonight that I should not feel any sort of way.

I am single.

I, Finnley Thompson, am single.

Chapter Sixteen

Brett

It's Saturday, and I only have two days off for the next week and a half. Scott is out on vacation, so I doubled up on shifts. He flew to Prague for the week. One could take a wild guess on why he decided to go there. The stupid goon thinks he will find a woman and somehow convince her to come back with him.

Too bad, Scott is not that lucky.

When I see my server, I flag her down.

"One more beer, please."

"You got it."

I watch as the young blonde walks off. She can't be more than twenty-one. Not much younger than Finnley. There I go again. Thinking about that feisty redhead. I've been avoiding her all week after worrying about her last weekend. I needed to distance myself. I couldn't understand why I was even worried. It was pathetic. I should not be worrying about someone I hardly know.

It's been six days since I have heard from her. I never responded to the last message she sent me and here I am, still thinking about her.

Popping a fry in my mouth, I look around the pub. Something unexpectedly catches my eye. Not something, but someone. It causes the hairs on the back of my neck to stand up.

There is no fucking way.

I squint in attempt to try to see a little better, clearer. It sure as hell looks like my baby brother.

My blood begins to boil and try as I might, there is no containing it. Not after what he did.

Without thinking, I stand and suddenly my server appears, blocking my view. She has returned with my beer. Too bad I no longer want it. Groaning, I sit back down.

"Is everything okay, sir?"

"Yeah," I say through gritted teeth. Nothing is okay. Not now, especially if that punk has returned to town.

My server clears her throat. "Sir?"

Fuck, she said something, and I was not paying attention.

"Could you repeat that? "

"Um, is there anything else I can get for you at the moment?"

"I'll take the check when you get a chance."

She looks at me in shock. "Of course. Can I get you a box?" The blonde points to my unfinished dinner. I hardly ate anything.

"That would be great."

My server nods and walks away fast. Gone is the figure who was standing a few feet away. Fuck. I lost him and it's probably best I don't go on a search for the asshole. Finding him would not end well.

As soon as my server returns, I exchange the container for my debit card. I need to get out of this place and fast.

I peel out of the Iron Rose Pub as quickly and legally allowed. If it was my dumbass of a brother and he just happened to be walking in the lot, I would be too tempted to run him down, and that would be frowned upon in my line of work. Plus, he is not worth going to prison for. The temptation to do so is there though. I will not lie.

I remind myself that he wasn't worth taking out back then and he sure as hell ain't worth it now.

As soon as I'm in the confinements of my home, I go straight for the cabinet. A bottle of bourbon awaits.

* * *

Squeezing my eyes shut, I only see two people. Abigail and my brother. The two of them naked in the bed I shared with her. My brother and my fucking wife.

I open my eyes to pour myself another shot. I fill the amber liquid to the rim, some of it pours over. Oops. I briefly wonder how many shots I have had.

Not enough if I'm still having visions of the two people I loved most in the world betraying me. The two of them fucking comes to the forefront. Always there, lurking. Reminding me of everything I lost.

Fuck them.

Taking the shot glass, I shoot it fast and pour another one.

I keep hearing a ringing sound. I try to ignore it, but it does not go away. Finally it stops and I feel like I am about to doze back off when I hear it again.

Fuck!

This time it stirs me from my groggy state and that is when I feel a vibration against my side. Reaching down, I feel my phone. My phone has been ringing and is currently ringing in my hand. I can barely make out the name.

Her name.

After three attempts at using the facial recognition, my phone finally unlocks. I think there are a ton of text messages and missed calls. However, my eyes are having trouble focusing. Fuck it, I decide. I will just deal with it all later. Between my eyes and head pounding and whatever the hell that smell is, I just can't.

When I finally manage to sit up, I tap the home screen on my phone. The time is just past midnight. I rub my face and glance around. I can see a little better. The first thing I notice is the bottle of bourbon. The bottle is almost empty. Next to the bottle is a tumbler with some amber liquid inside of it.

That is odd. Have I been drinking? I try to think but everything is fuzzy, and it makes my head spin more.

The ringing starts back up again. Finnley's name appears on the screen and somehow, I manage to answer.

"Hello?"

"Brett! Oh my gosh! I have been so damn worried! Don't you ever pull that shit again!" Finnley yells through the receiver, causing me to pull it away because fuck, my head hurts. What the hell has her so worked up?

"Do you hear me?"

"What, why are yelling at me?"

"What do you mean why am I yelling? You sent me a cryptic text message and then left me hanging. I have been worried you went and did something stupid."

I shake my head in confusion. I have no fucking clue what she is rambling about.

"Are you still there?"

"Yeah, yeah, I just, umm..." My words start to slur. I know what I want to say yet cannot seem to make myself say them.

It must be the bourbon.

"You're drunk!" she yells again into the phone. "That's it. Give me your address."

She's crazy. I am not drunk. Am I? I look back at the bottle. Okay, so maybe I am fucking toast. Regardless, I don't need her coming here. That's the last thing on earth that I need.

"I don't need a babysitter. I am fine."

"Is that so? Is that why you told me you wanted to fucking kill your brother? That you wanted your revenge?"

I sit there stunned silence. I would never say those thoughts out loud. Now I wonder if I said any other stupid shit in my drunken state. I pull my phone from my ear and try to open our texts. As I finally manage to open our texts, my phone pings with a notification. My fingers move faster than my brain and I hit accept before reading.

What was that?

From a distance I hear her yell, "Brett! I'm coming."

Fucking hell.

What did I just do?

Chapter Seventeen

Brett

"You better open this door right now! I know you're in there!"

Shouting and pounding come from the entry way. I sit up too fast and instantly regret it. I feel like I might get sick. My fucking head is killing me, and it starts to make my stomach churn.

I grab my head in a weak attempt to stop the throbbing. It does not stop and neither does the damn knocking.

Who the fuck is at my door?

"I am not leaving until you open this door. I need to see that you are okay."

Her voice.

It is her voice. I must be fucking dreaming. I close my eyes and picture her face, speckled with freckles. Her vibrant green eyes stare at me, haunting me.

"Brett!" her voice calls out for me. I swear this might be the best dream I have had in a long while.

Pounding comes again, stirring me back awake. "Brett, open this door, right now!"

She's here?

At my house?

"I'm coming!" Dammit. I stumble my way to the front door, nearly tripping over my own two feet.

It takes me a few tries to finally get the door unlocked and when I do, a very angry Finnley stands in front of me. Her arms are crossed, and her fiery red head is a mess.

"It's about damn time!"

I stand there, unsure of what to say. I don't even know why she's here.

"You are completely wasted." Finnley shakes her head and storms past me right into my house. I didn't even invite her in.

"What are you doing here?" I ask as I shut the door. I try to follow her, but everything is swaying. I see the entryway table and attempt to make my way to it. As soon as I reach out for it, everything goes black.

* * *

It's dark, yet I hear voices. Blinking a few times, I allow my eyes to adjust. I look around. I'm lying in my own bed. How did I get here and who the hell is in my house?

The second I sit up to reach for my gun that I keep in the nightstand, I'm met with intense pain that causes me to stop. My shoulder is on fire.

Fuck!

The question still remains: Who is in my house?

Forcing myself up, I open the drawer, but my gun is not there. Instant panic fills me. I shoot up and out of bed despite my body hurting the way it does.

When I reach my door, I stop and listen. There's is more than once voice, however they are muffled, and I can't make out what they're saying. I crack the door.

"All I am saying is, don't be surprised when he tries to push you away. It's all he knows how to do."

"Like I said, I can handle my own. Thanks for the tip though."

Finnley's voice. I recognize it immediately.

My head pounds with each step I take, but I make it to where the voices are coming from. I stop short when I spot them. To say I'm shocked when I see two people standing in my kitchen would be an understatement.

"Good morning, sunshine," Luke says with a smirk on his face.

"Finally! I was ready to call for an ambulance,

but your buddy here talked me out of it. Consider yourself lucky," Finnley says before taking a sip of whatever is in the mug she is holding.

I don't say anything as I try to process what's happening and how we got to this point. I vaguely remember her standing at my front door. I just don't know why she was there or how she even got there.

"Bastard is clueless. I told you." Luke chuckles as he pushes off the counter and walks up to me. He taps me on the shoulder. "She might be a keeper, try not to fuck it up. Oh, and your gun is locked in your case."

"How do you know?" I question.

"You texted me, dumbass."

Without another word he walks away, leaving the two of us alone. Neither of us say a word until the front door closes, confirming that he left.

"You really have no idea? You don't remember?"

I shake my head. "The only thing I know right now is that I have a headache."

Finnley rolls her eyes as if she is annoyed with me, which in return annoys me.

"What?"

"You really don't remember? That is just pathetic, and here I thought me getting drunk at the pub was bad. You are ten times worse."

I try to replay last night as I make my way

around the island. I need something to kill the pain. Along with water. I need water. As soon as I reach up to open the cabinet, I groan in pain and grab my shoulder.

"What happened to my arm?"

"Hmm, my guess would be that you hurt it when you fell. You know you passed out and hit the table by the front door on the way down. Nearly gave me a heart attack so I grabbed your phone and called Scott, but he didn't answer. I didn't know what to do so I opened your texts and saw the name below mine and called it."

"Wow."

I pass by Finnley to fill my cup with water, and she gasps.

"Ugh! You smell like death. I'm going to start you a shower."

"You don't have to do that."

"I know."

Two words. Those two words say so much more though. I know it as soon as our eyes meet.

Chapter Eighteen

Finnley

Turning the dial on the hottest setting, I let the water begin to fill his giant tub.

I try to focus on everything but the look Brett gave me while we were in the kitchen. It was intense. Too intense. Luke told me, well warned me, that Brett was damaged and broken and that it was not my job to fix him. Maybe I'm not fixing him. Maybe I'm helping him help himself.

I tell myself that I'm not getting attached. How could I when he is so closed off?

Yet, it doesn't stop me from wanting to bathe the man.

It is not long before steam to starts to fill the large space. There's a large walk-in shower. Two sinks, though it's obvious that only one is used.

The bathroom mirror begins to fog, and Brett

still hasn't come in. I go to get him but as soon as I hit the doorway between his bedroom and bathroom, there he is. I stop and just stare at the man.

Brett has both arms displayed out in front of him, leaning against his black dresser. His head hangs low. Even like this, looking completely broken, he is beautiful. He is all muscle. From his shoulders down to his stomach, muscles that seem to flex with each breath he takes.

I don't want to disturb him, but I bet he prefers hot water over cold.

"Brett," I whisper, and he immediately tenses.

He slowly turns to face me and when he does, I see it.

Vulnerability.

It is written across his face. There's no denying it.

"Come on before the water gets cold." I wave behind me.

I walk back into the bathroom and wait.

Brett walks in, pausing just inside the bathroom. He grabs the waistband of his olive green sweats. There's a logo in the top corner. What the logo is I don't know because right then he starts to lower his sweats. He hesitates, not pulling them down any further. I will myself to stop staring at the skin he has exposed. I look up at him and as soon as my eyes meet his, he drops his sweats the rest of the way. I want to look down, however, I refrain, keeping my eyes on his. The vulnerability is still there, along with something else. His blue eyes show me something like desire. It gives me chills.

Suddenly I start questioning my decisions. I'm not entirely sure if staying in here is a good idea.

Brett walks past me, allowing me to check him out without his eyes on me. Straight muscle. Perfect ass.

Brett's body is flawless. Seriously, it is amazing.

I watch how his glutes move as he steps into the tub. He turns, giving me now a full show of what he is made of.

What a sight Brett Hayworth is.

It's enough to turn a girl on and let me tell you, he has me all hot and bothered right now. The man isn't even touching me, yet here I am now horny.

He hisses as he dips down into the water. It snaps me out of my daze.

"Is the water too hot?"

"It's fine. I need this," he replies as he leans back, closing his eyes.

I watch the rise and fall of his chest. Do I stay or go? Shit. The visual I had mapped out in my mind looks nothing like the scene before me. He reeked and needed a shower. When I got in here and saw the tub, I figured that would be better. I tossed in some shower gel, creating some bubbles, so what do I do now?

"Um..." I start but am unable to form words.

"Are you going to bathe me?"

Brett's words catch me off guard. His eyes are still closed and if he didn't just speak, I would almost assume he was asleep.

Except he did speak.

And now I need to come up with something coherent to say.

"Washcloths are in the linen closet. Second shelf."

I nod. "Right, the washcloth."

I move a little too quickly toward the closet at the other end of his bathroom. As soon as I slide the door open, I pause. There are baskets on each shelf and each one is labeled. There is one for towels, washcloths, hand towels, toilet paper.

"Did you get lost?" Brett asks.

Looking up at him, his eyes are still closed.

"Coming." I hurry, reaching into the basket and grab a cloth. Maybe he has OCD. Bet that pairs well with his grumpy mood.

I walk up to him, holding the washcloth. I am a confident woman. Yet seeing him like this... I'm not sure I can wash him.

Brett Hayworth is naked under those bubbles.

He must feel my eyes on him. His eyes pop open and find mine. He stares, unblinking. It makes me feel things. Things I should not feel for a man who seems so broken.

I'm the first to break eye contact. I dip the cloth in the water, careful not to touch him, and then reach for the shower gel.

"I just need to add some soap."

Once the soap is on, I kneel. I scoop up what water I can with my hands and pour it over his head gently. I decide to start by massaging his scalp. His dark hair is short, but long enough that I can run my fingers through it.

After a few minutes, I pick the washcloth back up and start washing his neck, moving down to his shoulders. He is tense and occasionally, he flinches.

"Lean forward," I say.

Brett does as I say, and I continue washing his back, stopping just above his ass.

"You can sit back."

He sighs and leans back again.

Now to wash his front. My nerves have reached a new high. My hands tremble slightly as I take the navy cloth to his chest. It's so slight, I doubt he can feel it. Still, it makes me nervous, knowing the possibility is there.

I take my time washing his stomach. I repeatedly make circles, stalling. Do I wash his cock? Like, where is a damn guidebook when one needs it? Sure, I've showered with guys in the past, but it was far from intimate and not at all like this.

I tell myself washing his cock is no biggie. I mean, it might in fact be huge, but I shouldn't make this a big deal. I need to think of it as helping him.

Fuck it.

I dip the washcloth under the water. The second I feel him, he sucks in a deep breath. Meanwhile, I'm holding my breath because I can tell he is hard. He's fucking hard.

I glance up at him, his eyes are now tightly closed. It's as if I am causing him pain, even though that's not possible.

Neither of us says a single word.

Not one word.

It feels it takes eternity to wash him, when really it was less than a minute. I move on to his thigh.

Brett moves fast, grabbing me by my upper arms, pulling me over the side of the tub. It happens so quickly that I'm caught off guard.

A squeal leaves my lips but is quickly silenced by Brett's lips. His kiss is sloppy. His arms move all over my body, soaking my clothes to my bones. Without another thought, I do the same. My hands roam all over his body. I want to feel every ounce of his perfectly chiseled chest.

He is the first to break our kiss. He moves on to my neck, just below my ear. Goosebumps form. I want more of his mouth on me. I don't even care where he kisses me. As long as his mouth is on me in some way.

I sit back, breaking our contact with each other. We are both breathing heavy. Lust-filled eyes stare at me. I'm one hundred percent certain that mine look exactly like his.

I grab the hem of my top and pull it roughly over my head. With my shirt goes the claw clip that was holding my hair back. Messy red hair fans around chest, falling just above my black lace bra.

Water splashes over the side as Brett leans forward, kissing my collarbone. I can feel his erection as he trails kisses down to the top of my breast. He hesitates there for a moment, so I decide to help him out. I reach back and unclasp my bra.

Brett hisses as he watches the black lace falls disappearing under the bubbles.

I have no idea how far we will go.

What I do know is that I am going to enjoy the ride.

Chapter Nineteen

Finnley

Brett wastes no time. His hot breath fans my breast before his mouth envelopes my nipple. His teeth graze it ever so slightly. I arch my back in response. The sensation is electrifying.

Reaching under the water, I take his length in my hand. Not only is he rock hard, he's also thick. I stroke him while he continues sucking and nipping.

"Finnley," Brett breathes into my chest while his hand grips my other breast.

"Mmhm," I moan and lean back to look at him while continuing to run my hand up and down his cock.

"I... I haven't... I... it's been..."

He trails off, not finishing what he wanted to say. I arch an eyebrow but give him a sly smile. I am enjoying watching him slowly lose control.

With some space between us, I let go of him and stand. A moan leaves Brett's mouth and makes me giggle. Clearly, he is not happy with the loss of my hand.

It's okay though, because I reach for the waistband of my soaked yoga pants and yank them down. It's a little bit of a struggle because they are clinging to my skin.

There I stand in Brett's huge tub, naked with him staring up at me. Actually, he is staring at my bare pussy.

"Like what you see?"

Brett runs a hand through his hair. "Fuck, Finnley."

"Is that a yes?"

"The hell with it," he mumbles. And then just like that, his mouth is suddenly on my pussy. My hands fly to his hair with the first stroke of his tongue.

His tongue darts in and out, causing me to moan. I'm so fired up I don't think I will last. Especially if he keeps his current rhythm up. My legs are already starting to tremble.

"Brett, don't stop, please don't stop." I have zero control as my orgasm nears.

Brett does not stop. He doesn't stop when my legs shake uncontrollably. He doesn't stop when I scream out his name.

He only stops when my legs give out and I practically collapse on top of him.

Brett adjusts, allowing me to settle on top of him. His cock is now at my entrance. My body is still on fire so without thinking, I sink down slowly. A moan escapes my lips as I adjust to take all of him.

Our eyes meet and something flashes in his eyes. What we are doing is intimate, and I try to not focus on that part.

Just focus on the pleasure, Finnley.

My movements pick up when he takes a nipple in his mouth. My clit tingles again and before I know it, I come apart in Brett's arms.

Brett's release follows quickly behind mine. He thrusts hard before groaning in pleasure.

As soon as his breathing calms, he slides out of me. It leaves me feeling empty. All too fast, he starts moving out from under me. He is gentle with me though, setting me down in the now chilly water. He steps out of the tub, and I am still too far gone to pay attention to what he is doing.

Brett returns, lifting me out of the tub. "Here," he says as he wraps me in a fluffy white towel. He walks me over to his shower, removes the towel, and hangs it on the hook.

I step under the steamy spray, thankful that it is hot. He steps in behind me and runs his hands down my back. After a moment his hands leave my body but soon return, this time with a cloth.

Now it's his turn to bathe me.

How this took a three-sixty, I have no idea and I am certainly not going to complain about it.

I say nothing while he washes me. If I'm being totally honest, I'm unsure what to say. I came here to initially to make sure the man was okay. In no way did the thought of having sex with him ever cross my mind.

I close my eyes and lean my head back when Brett rubs the cloth over my sensitive parts.

"Hurt?"

"No, just a little sore."

"Are you on—"

"Yes, I have an IUD." I cut him off to save him from having to ask the awkward question. We just had unprotected sex. We are practically two strangers. I'm known to be spontaneous, just not to this degree.

"That's... that is good."

"And I'm clean."

Might as well get it all out of the way.

"Me too."

"Are you though? Hot single cop. Have you ever gone to get tested for anything?"

Brett moves onto washing my thighs and legs before speaking. Then he washes my feet and stands.

Still no words are spoken. And just when I think the man I just had sex with will not be answering my question, he clears his throat

"I am clean."

I turn to face him. He looks defeated. Maybe he regrets what just happened. Not my problem. I have no regrets.

I put my hands on his hard abs. "You sound so sure of yourself."

Brett takes a step back and my hands fall.

"I don't like to be touched."

Wow, that's a shocker. My hands were all over him not even an hour ago. I think I should take that as my cue to leave.

"Right. Got it. No touching." I turn and rinse my face once more before stepping out of his shower. I grab the closest towel and wrap it around me. When I go to reach for my clothes, I realize they are wet. Soaked.

"Fuck."

This is just fucking wonderful. I wanted to escape and fast Now that doesn't seem possible. I need to think of a plan and quick.

"Finnley, listen, it's not what you—"

I wave my hand at him. "No need to explain anything to me. I hear you loud and clear."

To hell with staying here, I'll drive home in his towel. I can mail it back.

I gather up my clothes and walk out of his bathroom. I've just made it to the living room when he calls out my name. I don't stop though.

"Dammit, Finnley, wait!" Brett calls out as I put my hand on the knob of the front door. His hand grips my shoulder, forcing me to turn and face him. He's wrapped in a towel himself. His hair is a mess, beads of water drip from the ends, landing on his shoulder and chest. And I'd be a liar if I said I wasn't turned on all over again. He has that freshly fucked look and I like it. But no, I can't like it. This is over.

"Look, Brett, we had sex. So what? Let's not make a big deal out of this. I'm not a stage five clinger. You don't have to worry about me blowing up your phone or stalking your place."

He groans out in frustration, running his hands through his hair. "You really want to know how I know I am clean?"

We are back to that?

"Sure." I put my hand on my hip. "Let's hear it."

"I haven't been with anyone since my wife."

My mouth falls open.

Oh hell, I sure was not expecting that. I knew he said he hadn't kissed anyone since her, but lots of guys don't kiss. This, though, this is different.

Way fucking different.

"Say something."

Yeah, I should totally say something. I lift my hand from my hip and start walking back toward the living room.

"Come on, I'll cook you something to eat."

Chapter Twenty

Finnley

"So, are you going to explain to me what caused you to go and get shitfaced?" I ask while dishing Brett up some scrambled eggs. It's almost one in the afternoon, but eggs are fine any time of the day.

Am I being nosey? Sure, but I deserve to know. He had me in a panic.

"It's a long story."

"Is it? Good thing I have the rest of the afternoon to hear it."

"I rather we just forget about it."

"Forget about it?"

'Yeah."

I watch as he takes a bite of his eggs, zero expression on his face. Like he thinks this will all be washed down the drain. The same way we washed the sex off each other, right down the drain.

"I don't think so. I want to know what set you off. Luke said he had a pretty good idea, but it was your story to share, not his. So, share away."

"Fucking Luke."

"Hey now, don't blame him."

Brett grumbles something under his breath. I can't make out what it was though and that annoys me. I am back to square one. I am getting nowhere.

I take the last sip of my coffee before bringing it to the sink. How did we go from hot passionate sex to this bullshit?

Because Brett is a closed book according to Luke. He did warn me after all.

Shaking my head, I sigh. "This was fun, you keep eating. I'll see myself out."

"You're leaving?"

"Uh, yeah. You don't seem to be open to discussing what brought me here in the first place, and I don't have the energy to pry a locked door." I continue walking, making sure to grab all my things. Not that I brought much. It was chaotic. Which reminds me. "I'll wash and drop these back off." I pull at the sweats he put on me after dropping that bomb. They are big, but I rolled the waist enough to make them work.

"What?" Brett asks again with what I'm assuming is a mouth full of food. I don't bother with a reply. Instead, I head for his bathroom to retrieve my clothes that are most likely still wet.

By the time I return, Brett is standing at the front door. His head is cast down. In a way it makes me feel sorry for him. He is seriously battling some internal shit.

"Don't tell me you are holding me captive." I walk right up to him.

Brett looks up at me. He still looks like shit even after a shower and some food.

"I, uh, I'm sorry."

"Don't be. I'm not."

And I'm not. I may have been worried and then angry at him, which led to sex, but I am not the least bit sorry.

Brett steps away from the door and opens it for me.

"Thank you," I say as I step over the threshold.

"For what?"

"For the sex." I smirk and give him a wink before walking away.

"You had sex!" Violet all but yells from across the table.

"Shh!" I whisper back, hoping none of the men in this place heard her.

Speaking of, I am not sure why I let Violet talk me into coming to this wine lounge. I prefer an actual winery. This place here is giving me creeper vibes. Like, I seriously feel like someone is watching me.

I take a sip of my Moscato and casually look around. There is nothing here that makes me want to be here. Even the wine is just eh.

"Come on, spill the beans. I want to know! Was he any good?"

I take another sip while contemplating if I should tell her the truth or go with a lie.

"Finnley, I need deets."

"Fine. The sex was great."

"That's it?" She looks at me like I've lost my mind.

Maybe I have.

I reach into my wallet and grab some cash. "Let's go, I'll tell you about the rest on the way to the pub. I can't take another minute in here." I throw the money on the table and get up without waiting for her to respond. I know she will follow because that means she gets the details on me and Brett. She lives for romance stories.

As soon as I get in Onyx, my phone dings. It's Tyler.

Shit.

We have talked a little here and there, but since I slept with Brett last week, I have been unsure of how I feel. Therefore, I was filing it in the back of my mind to deal with at a later date.

When I open his message, I'm a little surprised.

. . .

What is that supposed to mean? I shoot him a bunch of question marks and put my phone away before taking us to the Iron Rose.

Once seated I order my drink of choice and pull out my phone. A new text from Tyler awaits.

I hesitate before responding. His previous text struck me as odd and now this. I know I am single and sex with Brett was just that.

Sex.

No strings attached.

I type it out and hit send. I look up at Violet who is staring at me. "Was that Brett?"

Ugh. She looks like a hopeless romantic. I guess that's fair considering she writes romance novels. Her hands are placed under her chin while she patiently waits to hear me divulge my sex life.

"Tyler," I reply.

"Ooh, I forgot about him!"

"I haven't. I've just been avoiding him since everything happened with Brett."

"That's understandable. Which brings us back to Brett. Spill it." She bats her eyes all sweet-like.

"It started as me taking care of him. I was helping him nurse a hangover. I don't know what set him off. Anyway, I showed up, ran him a bath because he reeked horribly. Next thing I know, he's pulling me into the tub."

"Ooh, I like where this is going. Tell me more."

"I am sure you do. You'll probably add this to a scene in one of your books."

Violet winks. "That's a strong possibility."

Shaking my head, I tell her the rest of the story, including the part where I thanked him for the sex.

"That part is totally going in one of my books!"

I laugh and glance at my phone. Two texts pop up from Tyler.

> Tomorrow

> Are you seeing someone else

The second text catches me by surprise. What would make him ask that? It's both odd and unsettling. There is no way he would know that I have been with Brett. Unless he was stalking me, and I highly doubt Tyler would do such a thing.

I start to type and then end up deleting my text several times. Finally, after chewing my lip, I come up with a simple reply.

> I am single.

> Tomorrow after five, I am free.

It's not a lie. I have zero ties to Brett. I also have zero ties to Tyler at this point.

I set my phone down.

"I'll be right back, I need to use the bathroom."

Violet waves me off, she is looking at something on her phone. Probably storing my story for future reference.

When I come out of the bathroom, I pass by the bar. It's packed, yet there's no way I could miss those eyes. Those beautiful blue eyes are locked on mine. I stop in my tracks.

Seeing him almost takes my breath away. It's the first time I have seen him since I walked out of his house. I won't lie, it makes me feel something. My heartrate picks up.

Unsure of what to do, I smile and wave. He gives a subtle wave back, that's it.

I take that as a hint and force my feet to move. I continue back to Violet. When I reach our booth, a hand grabs my wrist.

"Finnley."

The way he says my name sends chills down my spine. Dare I say that I like the way he says my name?

I turn to face Brett and boy when I do, I'm a goner. His scent. It is delicious. Something mixed with a woodsy aroma. He looks sexy as hell too. He is wearing a plain black shirt and a pair of faded jeans.

"Hi," I say.

"Hi."

Brett looks nervous while still holding my wrist. I look down at where our bodies touch before looking back up at him.

"So, who is this? You never introduce me to the guys you meet."

Shit! I forgot Violet was right there. When I

turn back to her, she is all wide eyed and smiling. Great.

"Guys as in multiple?" Brett asks suddenly.

I whip my head back to him fast, my red hair bouncing all over. There is a tic in his jaw.

Damn Violet. I swear I could kill her.

"Oh, you know Finley, she is drop dead gorgeous. All the men want her."

"I see." He nearly grits his teeth. "And how does Finnley handle all these men?"

Brett is practically glaring at me. I'm not sure if he is mad or jealous. The thought of either has my heart pounding in my chest. Neither should excite me, yet I am.

I raise my head to him and smile my best smile. "I allow them one date. If they are lucky and treat me right, they might get a second date." I wink, knowing this will get under his skin.

"Finnley," he grinds out.

"Brett, why are you here?" I ask.

"I was watching the game."

"No, I mean why did you follow me?"

He goes silent. His eyes lock on mine again. This time he shows me all the things he will not say. I want to scream, "Just say it!" But I don't. I know I will not get anything else out of the man. Not here. Maybe not ever.

I nod even though I really don't understand his

ways. When the silence becomes too much, I speak up.

"You should get back to your game. Don't want to miss a good play."

He sighs, dropping my wrist. I look down and instantly feel cold where his hand just was.

"Have a good night, Brett," I say quietly.

He nods and walks back in the direction of the bar. I sit down and put my hands in my face.

That was such a disaster.

Why is he so damn closed off? Why?

"He's hot!" Violet says, causing me to look up other.

"He's hot all right, but he has some demons or something. He is always grumpy."

"Well, if anyone can get a guy to open up, it will be you. You have that gift."

Yeah. She's right. I'm just not sure I'm up for the challenge.

Chapter Twenty-One

Finnley

It's almost time to meet up with Tyler. My wild red curls are thrown up in a messy bun on top of my head. I'm wearing a plain white t-shirt, navy joggers, and sneakers. Yup, minimal effort. I figure this is one way to test Tyler's worth. After his odd text, I'm not quite sure what to think about him. Hopefully this dinner will make or break me seeing him again.

As soon as I walk up to the hostess stand, the woman steps out from behind it. "Right this way." She smiles brightly at me. "You know, he said you were a gorgeous redhead, but that just doesn't do you any justice. I think you are absolutely breathtaking."

"Thank you." I continue following her while trying to process the fact that Tyler gave a description of me. It makes me feel good to know he thinks those things of me. On the other hand, her words hold a little more meaning. I am dressed in plain clothes and no makeup.

I spot Tyler seated at a far corner table. No one else is around. I wonder if this was at his request. I don't mind being seated away from others, though I am curious to know if he played a part in it.

Tyler stands and holds out my chair for me.

"Thanks," I reply as the hostess leaves us.

"You're welcome. How was your day?" Tyler's eyes look me over more than once. It gives me some sort of vibe that I am unsure of.

"My day was fine."

He nods and picks up his menu. "The avocado BLT is good."

"Hmm," is all I give while looking over the menu myself.

We sit in silence for a few minutes before I close my menu.

"Are you getting the BLT?"

I study him, completely baffled as to why he would assume I am picking that just because he said it was good. One of the things about being a confident woman is that I am fully capable of choosing my own meal.

"No, I am going with the buffalo chicken wrap."

"Oh."

I can't be certain, but I think I hear annoyance

in his voice. If that's the case I need to squash this shit now.

"Is that okay, Tyler?"

"What? Oh, yeah, yeah. I just wanted you to try it."

I sit there and study him momentarily before deciding it is not to dwell on it. It is best to move on.

As soon as our food order is taken, I decide to ask the one question that has be on the tip of my tongue since I sat down.

"You sent a few odd texts yesterday. Can you explain them?"

He looks up at me with a blank expression. I know the man isn't going to play dumb with me.

"You know, the I thought we had something going, and asking me if I am seeing someone texts." I raise an eyebrow while watching him process my words. His blue eyes hold secrets. That much I can tell.

What kind of secrets? That question remains unanswered.

Tyler swallows slowly. "I, uh, I just felt like you might be talking to someone else."

"What makes you think that? Did I give you some kind of inkling that I was dating someone?"

"Yes, I mean no. No, you didn't. I just assumed."

"Tell me something, Tyler, are you an insecure guy?"

"What? No!"

Ah, there it is. He most definitely has some issues. Hmm... what to do with this information? I take a few sips of my water while debating on where to go from here. I can't do insecure.

"Listen, I am going to be straight with you. I am a very independent woman. I do not do well with guys who assume things due to their own personal issues. I'm not saying you are wrong for whatever issues you have, but I do not have time to explain myself repeatedly. As of today, right now, I am a single woman. I am tied down to no one."

Tyler grabs the back of his neck, clearly unsure of what to say to my oh-so-blunt statement. It sends us into an uncomfortable silence.

Lucky for him though, our food arrives shortly after, saving him from having to respond to that.

Or maybe it's lucky for me. Right now, I'm not sure.

* * *

"Can I see you again?" Tyler asks as he walks me to my car.

I smile, shrugging my shoulders. He is hot after all. His messy light brown hair falls in his eyes and he brushes it back. It's the other stuff that has me unsure.

"Maybe," I say, unlocking Onyx.

I go to open the door, and suddenly Tyler moves in close. It catches me off guard. Those flight or fight instincts kick in when he lifts his hand to my face. As quick as they came, they start to fade when he tucks a loose curl behind my ear.

"You are beautiful."

"Thank you."

Without another word Tyler leans in, kissing me. He kiss is soft at first, but the second his tongue slides in my mouth, it grows rough. He kisses me aggressively, like he is trying to claim me or something. I don't like it. When I got to pull back, his hand finds my head and he holds me in place. Suddenly a feeling forms in the pit of my stomach, and not the kind that gives a girl butterflies when she kisses a guy for the first time. No, this is the complete fucking opposite.

Placing my hands on his chest, I push him hard.

He stumbles back and puts his hands up. "What the hell was that for, Finnley?"

He's joking, right? He must be as I stand there in complete disbelief.

"Well?" he snaps.

Nope, not joking. This guy is pissed, and it shows me a side of him I do not like.

"I tried to catch my breath, and you held me there like a caged animal!" I cross my arms. I should not be explaining myself to this dude at all. No way. If anything, he is the one who owes me an explanation.

I shake my head. "Why don't you tell me what the fuck you were doing, thinking that was acceptable?"

He runs his hands through his hair. I hate that I like it when he does it.

"I was just kissing you, caught in the moment, you know."

"No, I don't know. Caught in the moment should be consensual between both."

"I... you are right. It is just, you are so fucking hot. I thought you wanted it."

He still looks angry, yet his words sound remorseful. Regardless, I don't like how he just acted and now he is turning it around like it was my fault.

"I need to go." I open my door to get in. Tyler reaches quick and grabs my wrist.

"Wait."

"What?" I snap while looking at him like he has ten heads because he must to be some sort of crazy to think I still want to be here with him. Alone in a parking lot no less.

"You're not mad, are you?"

"No, Tyler, I am not mad. I am turned off by

your aggression. Now, if you'll excuse me, I need to go."

He steps back while once again running his hands through his hair. Hot or not, he is clearly bad news.

"Good night," he says in a last-ditch effort to smooth shit over before I shut my door, locking it right away.

By the time I get back to my place there is a text from him. I regret opening it instantly.

> I'll call you tomorrow. I'd like to see you again.

Fucking hell.

Chapter Twenty-Two

Brett

I have received several texts alerting me that my piece of shit brother is back in town. Minus her of course. She has yet to be spotted.

"Dude, why don't you just fucking call her? You know you want to."

I hate when Luke starts throwing out the questions. I take a sip of water. Ever since the night I got shitfaced, I haven't touched a drop of alcohol. Can't go there again. I refuse to.

"Well, fucker?" Scott chimes in as he gets up. Probably going back to the bar to flirt with the bartender.

I shrug. "I don't know. I don't think I am ready. Besides, I probably scared her off."

"Scared her off, you can't be serious. I saw the

way she looked at you when she saw you last week in the pub. She has a thing for you."

"Maybe she does. Like I said, I'm not sure I am ready..."

"Stop with that woe is me bullshit. It's time to move on from Abigail. She ain't coming back, and even if she did, I wouldn't let you go down that path."

Luke might have good intentions, but I wish he would just drop it. Knowing him though, he won't.

"Look at yourself, Brett. You fell to an all-time low and Finnley didn't bat an eye. She stayed there by your damn side. I can't name many chicks that would do that. Fucking nursed you back to health. I think you got a good one. At least see her again. Don't let her go."

I hate to admit that he has a point. A pretty fucking valid one.

"Fine, I'll ask her out again. Will that get you off my back?"

Luke laughs. "I'm just watching out for you, man. It's time to put the past where it belongs. Behind you."

"Fine, all right. I'll reach out."

"That's better. You should try getting laid too. It will probably help your mood."

"Fuck off." I give nothing away. I haven't told a soul about what happened between Finnley and me. No plans to either. For one, I don't think

Finnley would appreciate me sharing. Two, the guys would have a fucking field day. I shake my head imagining what they would say. Taking my cell out of my pocket, I open up until I find her name.

How have you been?

I get a response back almost immediately.

Just got back from a shitty date.
How are you?

She went on a date? This shouldn't come as a shocker. I mean, Finnley is every ounce of beautiful.

I don't like it though. The fact that she went out with someone else. Not one bit. I do my best to conceal any annoyance while digging for more information.

> What was so bad about it?

> It started out okay, but at the end of the night he kissed me and became aggressive over it.

> Such a turn off.

She was forced to kiss some guy? I try to contain the anger that is building, but Luke must notice.

"Yo man, what has you all pissy now?"

I look up mid-text. "Finnley went on a date tonight. The asshole forced her to kiss him."

"You serious? We got a name for this fucker?"

"That's a good question." And one I intend to get out of her.

I go back to my conversation with Finnley.

> Who was this clown?

> No one important. I won't be seeing him again.

> I'm coming over

I slide my phone back into my pocket without waiting for her to respond. I want his name, and I plan to get it.

I stand as Scott comes back. He has a smirk on his face.

"I got myself a date."

"That's nice. I gotta go"

"What? Where are you going?"

"Finnley's."

As I walk away, I hear the two of them talking. Luke gives him a recap of what I just told him. Hearing it sets my blood boiling. Who in the hell?

I pull up outside of her complex a little after ten-thirty. As I get out of my truck, I spot a person hovering in the stairwell. From here, I can't tell if it is a guy or girl. Whoever it is, is dressed in dark clothes and wearing a dark beanie.

I approach slowly, quietly. When I get a little closer, I can see that they are looking at something on their cell phone. I continue walking slowly, until I step on something. A piece of plastic maybe. It crinkles beneath my boot. The person looks up fast, and suddenly jumps to their feet.

"Woah!" I call out. One hand is on my waistband, where my holster is concealed.

They take a step forward. They seem only hesitant once the light barely hits their face. A male.

Before I know what's happening, the guy turns and runs up the stairs. I quickly chase after him. By the time I reach the top of the stairs, he is nowhere in sight.

"Fuck," I whisper.

I take a moment to contemplate what to do next. Do I call in a suspicious person? I mean, they could live here in the complex for all I know. However, the dark clothing and running away doesn't sit well with me.

I decide to call it in. Better safe than sorry.

After waiting for the arriving officer, I give a replay of what went down. Another officer arrives and they head off to survey Finnley's apartment complex.

Finnley.

Shit.

I almost forgot what I was doing here in the first place. When I reach her door I send a quick text.

> Are you still awake?

> Uh yeah, you said you were coming over. It would be rude to go to bed.

I swear this woman and her wit.

> Open the door

. . .

Less than a minute later, Finnley opens the door. I am nearly blown away by the sight of her. Red curls frame her porcelain skin. Her face is free of makeup, putting her freckles on display. Freckles that beg to be kissed.

"Well, are you just going to stand there?"

I blink twice before snapping out of it. I nod and follow her into her apartment. As soon as the door shuts, I lock it.

Finnley plops down on the couch. She's not wearing a bra, that much I can tell.

"So, Brett, what brings you here?"

I came to get the asshole's name, except now that I am here, I think I might want more than just that.

I swallow slowly before answering the beauty in front of me.

"What is his name?"

Finnley shakes her head while laughing sarcastically.

"What's so funny?" I find nothing funny about some guy forcing himself on a woman. Especially with it being Finnley. I try to tell myself I am not developing feelings for her.

After all I built a wall around my heart. There is no way feelings for her are possible.

"I'm laughing because you come over here acting all cop like, wanting the dude's name."

"Finnley, I am a cop."

"His name does not matter. I will not be seeing him again." She waves a hand in the air. "So now that you are here, want to watch a rom-com and eat junk food?"

I don't know how she does it, but the woman effectively ends the conversation about her date. When I don't respond, she huffs and playfully hits my chest.

"Oh, come on, Brett, you didn't really come all the way here just to get my date's name, did you? That's something you could have done by text. You could have saved yourself the gas."

I move without thinking. My brain no longer works the way I need it to. I lean in and grab the back of Finnley's neck, pulling her to me. The second our lips touch, she opens for me. She does not waste any time climbing onto my lap. Our kiss deepens while she runs her hands through my hair. My dick twitches as she scrapes her nails along my scalp. I know she feels it because she grinds against me. Her sexy little movements cause my dick to harden.

She is the first to pull back, but only slightly. "What was that for?" Her lips brush against mine.

Truth be told I am not entirely sure. "I'm not... I had this urge to kiss you."

Way to sound like a dumbass.

"Thanks for erasing that shitty kiss from earlier." Finnley starts placing little kisses on my lips until I grab her ass with both hands to slide her closer. From the moment her lips seal over mine, our kissing turns frantic as if we cannot get enough of each other.

"I want you," she half-whispers. She leans back and in one swift move, she yanks her top over her head.

Fuck.

I was right. She is not wearing a bra. Her perky breasts are practically in my face. I waste no time grabbing one and twirling her nipple between my fingers. Finnley whimpers as she brings her lips back to mine while pulling at my shirt. I reluctantly drop my hand from her breast to allow her to pull my shirt off.

As soon as it's off, my hands are back on her soft skin. I take her nipple into my mouth, she moans out, pulling at my hair. Her hands are all over me, only stopping when they land on my cock. She grabs me through my jeans. She pulls at them, fumbling with the button and the zipper.

"Brett..." She trails off while continuing to mess with my jeans.

It takes my brain a few to catch up with what is happening. Hell, it has been so fucking long since I have been intimate with anyone. What happened previously with Finnley happened on a whim, and I'm pretty sure I was still half drunk.

"Brett, a little help here."

I nod and lift her off my lap. She stands in front of me as I remove my shoes and socks. As soon as I start to pull my jeans down, her hands are on them, yanking them down.

"A little impatient, are we?" I joke.

All jokes go out the window the second she grabs my erection. Finnley's silky fingers slide up and down my length. Fuck if it doesn't feel good. Almost too good. If she keeps this up, there is a good chance I will blow my load in her hand. Especially while watching her, watching what she is doing to me.

"Finnley," I say through gritted teeth.

Gorgeous green eyes flick up to mine. She smirks as her hands land on my chest. She gives a little shove, pushing me back down on the couch. I watch, mesmerized as she slowly slides her red lounge shorts down. No panties.

A very naked Finnley stands in front of me.

Very fucking naked.

I'm face to face with her bare pussy.

I grab her hips, pulling her to me. For the second time tonight, my brain does not seem to function.

I have the sudden urge to taste her, and I do just that. I waste no time swiping my tongue along her slit. I tease Finnley's pussy with my tongue, and she grabs a hold of my hair. My fingers dig into her skin as I find a rhythm between flicking and sucking. It does not take long for her to start grinding into my face while she frantically pulls at my hair. It stings, but I am fucking enjoying what I am doing to her.

The minute she starts begging me not to stop, I know she is on the verge of losing control. I suck a little harder. Flick a little faster.

"Brett!" Finnley screams out my name as her orgasm rips through her. Her pussy pulsates against my mouth. Fuck if she doesn't taste divine.

Out of nowhere, Finnley pushes my head back and practically jumps on my lap. She straddles me as she lines herself up perfectly and sinks down on my dick in one swift motion. She wastes no time.

"Hell, woman," I say through gritted teeth.

"I know," she pants as her soft lips land on mine.

Finnley rides me, bouncing up and down on my dick. I sit back and take it. Not that I have much say in the matter. Even if I did, I wouldn't stop her. No way in hell. She feels way too good.

She arches her back as she continues riding me. With her tits practically bouncing in my face, I take one in my mouth. Little moans leave her mouth.

When my balls begin to tighten, I know the end is near.

"Finnley, I'm close."

She must not hear me. Her eyes are squeezed shut. Head still back. If she did hear, she ignored me.

"Finnley, not gonna last," I say between pants.

Still, she does not stop. No, instead, she grips my shoulders tighter.

Without warning, her pussy tightens around my dick. She begins riding me harder, faster.

"Fucking hell!" I grit out as I try to lift her off me before I lose it.

At the same time, Finnley's legs squeeze my thighs. She starts moaning loudly, her release ripping through her. She rides me hard while screaming out the Lord's name.

No longer able to hold back, I explode. My own release fills her as she rides out her orgasm. She milks every ounce of cum straight out of my dick. She leans her head on my chest while she catches her breath.

After a few minutes, Finnley leans up and looks at me. "That was amazing."

I stare at her in disbelief.

"What?" she asks with her eyebrow raised.

"Amazing?"

"You didn't think so?" She leans back as if she is offended.

"It was more than amazing." And that is the truth.

"I'm going to shower, you are welcome to join me." She winks as she climbs off my lap. I look down and catch my cum dripping out of her pussy. I'm turned on all over again and feel this urge to claim her as mine.

Maybe it is time.

"I'll be right behind you."

She saunters away, pulling her red hair down.

How the fuck did all this just happen? I came here to get some asshole's number.

Chapter Twenty-Three

Finnley

I hear Brett's feet as I step under the spray of warm water. It feels good against my skin.

That's twice now.

Twice that I have had sex with Brett.

Twice that I have rode his cock.

Twice that he has come inside me.

That last bit is not lost on me, and while I did not mean for it to happen intentionally, it still happened.

"Let me wash you," Brett says as he steps into the shower behind me.

And now make that twice that we have showered together.

I stay where I am, not facing him as he begins to wash my body. His gentle hands run the cloth over me until he reaches between my legs.

I pull back slightly. I am sore. Don't get me

wrong, it is a good sore. One I will gladly do again and again because sex with Brett is A-MAZING. For a stone-cold cop, his cock is nice.

"Are you in pain?"

"Not really. Just sensitive."

He says nothing more for the duration of our shower. Not even when I turn around to wash him the same way that he has me.

The silence starts to eat at me. Does he regret what just happened? I mean, oh well for him, because I sure don't regret it. Maybe he's worried about me being clean or on birth control. I mean after all, the guy hardly knows me. We are just two strangers who seem to have spontaneous sex.

Only when we step out of the shower does Brett speak.

"It's late, I should probably get going."

I look him up and down. He has my yellow towel wrapped around his waist. Little water droplets are still splattered about his chest. Even though we just had sex, I want more of him.

"You're welcome to stay the night."

Brett stands there and just stares at me. It's evident that he's surprised by my words.

I shrug as I turn. "Ball's in your court." I let go of the towel that I have wrapped around me and keep walking. I'm horny and will not deny it.

I make it to my bed before Brett grabs my hips, stilling me.

"Finnley," he breathes into back of my neck. I can feel his erection against my ass.

"Brett."

"Are you teasing me?"

I turn to look over my shoulder at him. "No. I meant every word I said."

Brett nods and I watch as his eyes roam over my body. My pulse quickens. He pushes me slowly face down on the bed. He skims his hands over my bare skin. My skin heats where he just touched. The second his fingers sweep over my lips, I arch my ass into him. I know he can feel how wet I am.

Brett takes his time though. He dips one finger and then another into me very slowly. Grasping at the sheets on my bed, I buck. I need him to touch more, faster. This is agony.

My entire body is on fire with need. I don't think I can take much more. I can feel myself tightening around his fingers.

"Brett, please," I moan into the sheets.

Just when I think I can see the fireworks beyond the horizon, he removes his fingers.

"Hey." I sound crazy while I begin to turn over to face him. However, he puts a firm hand on the middle of my back that prevents me from doing so.

"Stay still." His words cause me to stop moving right away. He takes one of his legs and spreads my legs further apart. He comes closer. I can feel his cock right there. Ever so slowly does he rub his cock along my very wet slit. Tormenting me in the very best way.

"Brett, I need— "

He doesn't let me get the rest of my sentence out. He slides in slowly, silencing me. He finds a slow rhythm, one that is both torturous and delicious.

"Fuck, you feel so good. Sex with you is incredible."

I know, Brett. I know.

My legs start to tremble. He must notice because he picks up his pace. Thrusting harder and faster. I squirm underneath him. The sensation is too much.

I scream out as I lose control. Fireworks explode. I swear I see brightly colored starbursts. I never want it to end.

This is pure ecstasy.

Once I finally start to come back to my senses, Brett is thrusting into me hard, filling me. It sets me off all over again. My overly sensitive parts have me screaming his name into the sheets as I come again. I'm clawing at anything my hands touch.

Just when I think I can't handle his cock in me another second, he slowly pulls out of me.

Brett leans against me but is careful not to put his weight on me. My skin is covered in sweat. I'm hot, yet cold.

He chuckles into my hair. "Did you get every-thing you needed?"

I turn my face. "What?" I'm confused.

"You started to say you needed something. Did you get what you needed?"

Oh! I huff and smile. "I did, thanks."

Now he has jokes. This is a new side of him, one I haven't seen before. I think I like it when he isn't so grumpy.

"Let me get something to clean you up with. I'll be right back."

When he returns, he does exactly as he said he would. He gently cleans me with a warm cloth. I can't help but flinch when he runs it over my swollen parts. Brett doesn't miss it and stops imme-diately.

"Am I hurting you?"

I shake my head. "It's a good hurt."

"Are you sure?"

"It is. Let's go to bed."

Brett nods and goes to put the cloth away. By the time he returns, I am under the sheets.

He climbs in next to me.

"What are you doing to me?" he asks quietly.

"I hope I'm breaking down those walls so that you'll actually let me in."

Chapter Twenty-Four

Finnley

By the time I wake up, I am alone. No sign of Brett remains.

When I go to check the rest of the apartment for him, I see the note that's been left on my kitchen counter.

Great.

I pick it up and read the words scribbled in pink ink.

> Finnley,
>
> I got called in to work early. I will call you later.
>
> Brett

I breathe a sigh of relief and set about making myself a pot of coffee. I honestly thought Brett threw up his shield and took off, that last night was too much. And maybe, in some ways, it was. However, I don't regret anything about it.

I probably should worry a little. Usually, people take it slowly. Not us, though. Nope, we dove straight into the deep end.

After downing one cup and pouring another, I go and grab my cell phone.

There's a message from Tyler. Ugh. I should just delete it, but curiosity gets the better of me.

Um, what? I feel the color drain from my face as I reread the words. A million questions start to swirl in my mind. The first one is, how the hell does he know Brett was over last night?

The second one is how does he even know Brett has a wife? Or had? Because of Tyler's text, now I'm not sure.

I pace from my kitchen to the living room and back again. I do it several times while trying to decide my next move. I have questions and I want answers. Honest fucking answers.

Ultimately, I decide to reply to Tyler first because I know Brett is at work. At least that's what he told me in the note.

What are you talking about?

When I don't get a response from Tyler, I head to start the shower. This shit is going to plague my thoughts until I get a response, and I don't have all day for this nonsense.

By the time I get out of the shower there is still no reply from Tyler. I would like to think he just sent some random bullshit text, except the mention of a wife leads me to believe it's not random.

I find Brett's name in my contacts and hit call. It rings and rings before going to voicemail.

Well, this is fun.

I have all these questions and not a single answer.

They say silence will eat a person alive and I believe it. The entire day, neither Brett or Tyler reach out. I go and get a mani-pedi. Pickup groceries, then come home and stress clean.

I am on the verge of going nuts when a knock sounds at my door. I jump at the sound.

As soon as I see the face on the other side of the door, I open it immediately.

"You didn't call me back!" I state with my hand on my hip.

Brett stands there in uniform. He looks sexy as hell too. Regardless, I want an answer.

He sighs as he steps into my place. "Every time I pulled out my phone to call you back, something came up."

"Was it because you were with your wife?" The words leave my mouth before my brain has a chance to catch up and stop me.

"What?" His blue eyes show a mixture of confusion and disbelief.

"I received a text. It asked me if your wife knew we were together. I need answers, Brett."

"Who the hell would send you that text?"

His normal husky voice is now full of anger. It only confuses my thoughts more. What if he's hiding something?

"Brett, I just need to know the truth." I try to sound confident, yet my words come out as a whisper.

"You think I'm married, Finnley?" His voice raises. "Do you see a tan line where my wedding band should be?" He holds up his ring finger.

I shake my head, unable to form any words.

"Let me ask you this. When you came to my house the night I was trashed, did my wife answer the door for you?"

"No, no." I shake my head while fighting to hold back my emotions.

"And when you stayed with me all night, did you notice any fucking pictures of my wife? Did she come home at all?"

Gone is the closed off and quiet Brett. In his place is an outraged man who is full of bitterness. It's clear that he's still battling demons left behind from his failed marriage.

His questions make absolute sense. I really had no reason to question him. Just that text.

"No, Brett. There were no signs. I just needed to know." I hope he hears the remorse in my voice.

"Who the fuck sent you that text?"

"Tyler."

Brett's entire body goes stiff at my words. If Brett wasn't pissed off before, he damn sure is now.

"Tyler sent you that text?!"

"Yeah, and I asked him what he was talking about but he never—"

Brett cuts me off. "Tyler! My brother, Tyler?! What are you doing talking to him?!"

Woah, what? Who said anything about a brother? I take a step back as his words slap me in the face.

"I'm sorry, what?"

Brett runs a hand down his face. He chest rises and falls erratically. "Who sent you the text, Finnley?"

"The guy I went on the date with."

"And what did you say his name was?"

"Tyler."

"Does this Tyler have a last name?"

I have to stop and think for a second. "Worth. I think that is what he told me."

"Worth, like Hayworth?" Brett asks. He takes a deep breath and closes his eyes. There's a tic in his strong jaw. He stays like that for what feels like forever before he opens his eyes. Instantly, I see the storm brewing in those blue eyes. A raging storm. One that is going to leave destruction in its path. I have a feeling--no, I know for certain that I am right in the center of that path.

"That's my fucking brother you're dating." Brett's all-too-calm words leave his mouth before he turns and storms out of my apartment.

His brother? How is that possible?

I don't suppose I'll get that answer tonight though.

Chapter Twenty-Five

Brett

I get in my cruiser and drive. Where to go, I'm not sure. I just need to drive, and I need to be away from Finnley. She does not need to see the mess that is my life. The look on her face when I told her she was dating my brother was more than enough to make me feel guilty. Even though I know it's not my fault, this feeling in my chest is heavy, and the last thing I need to do is lash out at her.

My fucking brother.

The fact that he mentioned Abigail to her has my blood boiling all over again. He used her to get to Finnley. For a moment, it worked because she questioned me. And boy, did it open an old wound. One I had been trying to stitch closed for a while. One that I thought might finally heal and scar over now that Finnley fell into my life.

But no, I am still just as raw as the day I caught the two of them together.

After driving for a while, I pull into my driveway and put my cruiser in park. I don't kill the engine right away, though. I try to wrap my head around this fucking shit show that seems to be my life. It doesn't take me long to start to put the pieces together.

Tyler is back in town. I had my suspicions a few weeks ago, now they are confirmed. It's obvious that he knows I'm seeing Finnley. Which means he is either watching me or watching her. Knowing my brother, he is probably watching both of us.

I slam my hand on the steering wheel. "Fuck!" This shit pisses me off to no end.

Killing the engine, I finally climb out. I scan my surroundings the entire walk up to the door. Tyler is a sneaky motherfucker. One that can never be trusted.

Once inside, I pull out my phone. There's a text from the fiery redhead.

Of course, there is.

Before opening her text, I send a quick text to both Scott and Luke, letting them know my piece of shit brother has in fact returned.

I'm not sure what I am expecting when I open Finnley's text, but the words on the phone screen are not it.

I didn't sleep with him

That woman. I hadn't even thought about that possibly. Fuck, just thinking about the two of them being intimate has me seeing red. The fact that she felt the need to make it known speaks volumes. I appreciate her telling me too. I won't lie, now that the thought has crossed my mind, I am relieved that they haven't slept together because it would ruin what we do have.

I start stripping out of my uniform while my brain continues going a hundred miles an hour. All the shit that's happened plays over and over.

I realize I need to explain some important details to Finnley. She knows my wife left me, that is all. At the time I didn't feel it was necessary that she know more. Hell, who wants to talk about the reasons their marriage failed? I am just pulling on a pair of sweats when I stop dead in my tracks.

That fucker was the one who forced himself on her. Forced her to kiss him. He was the reason I rushed to her apartment. And suddenly a new realization hits. He was the fucker in the shadows. I have no doubt about that knowing what I know now.

Red hot rage fills me. My fist slams into the mirror that sits in the corner of my room. Shards of glass fly everywhere. I don't give a fuck. I hit it again and again. I feel it.

All the pain.

All the anger.

All the hurt.

Every feeling from the past three years is finally being set free.

Only when there are no more pieces of the mirror still intact do I finally stop punching it. My hand is covered in blood and will most likely need a few stitches, yet I don't care. Letting it all out felt good. Damn good.

I go into the bathroom to clean my hand up. When I put my hand under the warm water, it stings. Red runs down the drain. I leave my hand there for a few minutes until the water starts to run clear.

Surprisingly, my hand does not look bad. The cuts don't look deep enough to warrant a trip to the hospital.

Thank fuck for that.

After bandaging a few up cuts up, I pull back the comforter and climb into bed. I'll deal with everything tomorrow after I get some sleep.

The first person I'll be starting with is my brother.

Chapter Twenty-Six

Finnley

Pounding wakes me from my sleep. I sit up fast, but everything is dark. On instinct, I touch my face. I feel something super soft. My sleeping mask.

I pull it up and shake my head. Way to give yourself an almost heart attack. For a second I thought I had been kidnapped and blindfolded. I really need to stop watching all those true crime documentaries. The pounding continues and it puts me on edge.

When I reach the door, I don't say anything. Instead, I check the peephole.

It's Brett.

I must say it's a surprise. After last night, I figured we were done. That any progress I had made with this man was destroyed by the fact that I unknowingly was seeing his brother. I even texted him to clear up the fact that while I had seen Tyler a few times, we never slept together. When I didn't get a response to that, I assumed all bets were off the table.

As soon as I unlock the door, Brett pushes his way in.

"Good morning to you too," I state as I shut the door.

"I am not in the mood for your smart ass, and just what the hell are you wearing?"

I huff and look down at what I am wearing before looking back at him. "What's wrong with this?" I'm wearing a silky white teddy. Granted, it barely covers my ass, but I am in my own home after all.

Brett pinches the bridge of his nose, and I can't help but laugh at the man. It's not even noon and he is in a mood.

"Why are you even here, Brett?"

"We need to talk," is all he says as he turns, heading into my kitchen where he starts opening cabinets.

"Um, can I help you find something?"

"Coffee."

I stand on my tippy toes to reach the cabinet above the stove. The silky material rises above my ass. I can practically hear Brett swallow. It makes me giggle.

Did I mention that I am not wearing anything under my teddy?

I feel him come up behind me. A hand grazes my cheek just as I grab the canister that holds the coffee. So much for needing to talk. I like the way his hand feels on my skin. I allow his hand to wonder more because I sure could use the distraction. The second his finger dips into me, he lets out a low growl.

"Brett."

"Shh, don't say anything."

That comes as a surprise. Even for him. Brett is not a go with it kind of guy.

His fingers continue to tease me. My heart rate rises. It feels good, and for a moment I allow myself to get lost in it.

Until I remember that Brett came here to talk. Fucking me with his fingers was most definitely not on his radar. Not with the way he was pounding on my door not even ten minutes ago.

"Brett," I say more sternly this time. His fingers freeze. "You came here to talk. Let's talk. I'll make coffee."

Somehow, I find the will to sidestep away from him. I go about making the coffee without a second thought.

"You're mad?"

I turn to see him with a confused expression across his face.

"Of course not. Believe me, I would love to pick up where we have left off; however, I think we have more important things to chat about."

Brett takes a moment, processing every word I just said. I mean, he probably is because that is how the man operates.

"Look, let's just talk about Tyler and we'll go from there."

His face changes instantly, as if someone hit a switch. "Right, my brother." He pauses. "I need all the information you have on him."

I sigh, I should have known this was coming. I too have my own set of questions. Ones Brett will have no choice but to answer.

Pouring the first cup, I hand it to him. "Sugar is in there," I point to the same cabinet that I pulled the coffee out of. "If you want hazelnut creamer, it is in the fridge."

"Black is fine."

Of course. Black just like his grumpy soul.

I say nothing as I pour my cup and grab the creamer from the fridge. Once my cup is to my liking, I speak.

"I will tell you whatever I know, but I need some answers first."

"Finnley, are we really doing this now?"

"Yes, we really are. Why did Tyler mention your wife to me?"

He groans out of in frustration, not answering me.

"Seriously, you are going to have to open up and let me in."

I watch as Brett takes a drink of his coffee. His eyes are closed. I so badly want to walk up to him and just shake him. Knock some things around up there, you know? I'm almost willing to do anything at this point in order to get the man to open up.

When his eyes open, gone are the baby blues I enjoy seeing. In their place are eyes so haunted that it gives me chills.

"Brett?" I half-whisper.

"Tyler is my baby brother. I took him everywhere with me when we were kids. When I got my license, he was my co-pilot. I never left him behind." He pauses to take another drink. "One day I went to pick Tyler up from school. He was standing there with a girl. He asked if we could give her a home.

"Later when I asked about her, he said they were just friends. She was a cheerleader, smart, and pretty. Tyler was a bit of a loner. On the edge of doing stupid shit. They were complete opposites, yet Abigail kept coming around." Brett swallows thickly before continuing. "The days turned to months and then years. Tyler started getting into more trouble. Petty trouble like stealing candy from gas stations, mouthing off to teachers. I was in the police academy and couldn't be around all the time. I don't know if that was why he was doing it. To this day I wonder if he was acting out to get back at me for leaving him behind."

"Where were your parents?"

"My parents worked around the clock. They weren't around much and when they were, they were sleeping."

"I see."

"I tried talking to Abigail one evening about it, to get her opinion on what was going on with my brother..." He trails off, staring blankly at my white kitchen cabinets.

Deciding it would be best that I don't interrupt his thoughts, I begin making my breakfast. By the time I throw a pop-tart in the toaster, he speaks.

"The next thing I knew, she was kissing me."

"Oh boy," I state as I pull the pop tart out at lightning speed because it is so damn hot. I plop it on the plate and turn to look at him.

"Who was I to deny her? I am a man after all. I had my own needs and wants, as selfish as that might sound."

"No wonder your brother is pissed. You were messing with his girl."

Brett slams his hand down on the countertop. "Abigail was not his girl!"

"My bad, relax. I was only trying to joke with you. You're always so grumpy."

"Me, grumpy?" He points to his chest. The storm now evident in his eyes. "The night we kissed was the start of the beginning of the end for us. We both made sure Tyler was okay with our relationship. He was my best man the day I got married. He was also the man I caught in my bed with my wife."

Holy shit! His words cause me to choke on my breakfast.

"I got off shift early to surprise Abigail for her birthday. When I walked in, it was quiet, except for mumbled noises coming down the hall. With my hand on my holster, I walked toward our room. The closer I got, the clearer the sounds became." He lets out a deep breath before swallowing. "My wife was moaning out Tyler's name. She was fucking screaming his name. I pushed the door open to find her on our bed riding my brother's dick reverse cowgirl. Tyler did not notice me at first, but the second Abigail came down from her orgasm, her eyes opened, and I was the first thing she saw.

Now you know why I am so damn grumpy."

"Brett, I... I am... I had no idea. I am sorry."

"The worst part is, as my brother rushed out of our home, he stated that it's always been him that she wanted. Later, I asked my wife about what he said while she packed her things. Finnley, Abigail looked me dead in the eyes and admitted that it had always been Tyler. She only chose me because I had my shit together. I meant nothing to her, while she meant everything to me."

He might as well rip my heart out and stomp on it. And here I was talking to, dating his brother. Fuck.

I walk over to him, throw my hands around his neck, and kiss his cheek before leaning into his ear. "I only went on a few dates with him. Aside from him forcing himself on me, that was as far as things went."

He pulls me back, keeping both hands on my arms. "You are to stay away from him. Far fucking away."

"I plan on it. After our last encounter I was done."

It takes him a minute, but it quickly registers. It's as if I flicked on a light bulb. Brett went from seriously hurt to pissed off real quick.

"So it was Tyler who forced himself on you?!"

"Yes."

"What the fuck!" Brett slams both hands on the counter. His rage roars.

"I didn't know he was your brother." I am not sure why I say it. Maybe it was the need to make it clear. I had no idea Tyler and Brett were even related. Sure, they both have blue eyes, but that is it. Their personalities are polar opposites.

"I didn't know," I whisper once more.

He pulls me back into his arms and studies me. Trying to gauge my honesty, I'm sure.

"I mean it, Finnley, after I get what I need you will be blocking all forms of communication. He is not someone you need to be getting caught up with. He destroys everything he comes in contact with. I will not have him taking you down."

I nod. I know his words hold nothing but the truth. Thinking about the strange texts from him and the way he forced me to kiss him. It gave me a bad feeling. It suddenly dawns on me.

"Brett, how does Tyler know I've been with you?"

He pulls back and meets me with this puzzled look. "What do you mean?"

"When he sent me the text, he obviously knew you were here with me."

"Okay?"

"Tyler doesn't know where I live. I never brought him here. Not once."

If I didn't know Brett was angry before, he sure is now.

He runs a hand down his face in frustration.

"Finnley, I need all the details on him. Now."

Chapter Twenty-Seven

Finnley

Brett is worried about me staying at my apartment alone. I mean, I understand his concern. We don't know where Tyler saw the two of us together. We could have been out to dinner for all I know.

I gave Brett everything I knew about Tyler. From his dating app information to his cell phone number. I even gave him a description of what he looks like since it has been well over a year since Brett has seen him face to face.

That was three days ago.

As I'm walking out of a new family practice that will be opening soon, I take one look at my car and immediately notice something doesn't look right. The hairs on the back of my neck stand up and I feel my face pale as I run up to Onyx.

No!

I circle my Camero. Someone has keyed it, and I'm not talking about running a line along my car.

It is worse.

So much worse.

The word WHORE is engraved in all caps in my hood. SLUT appears on the passenger door. On my driver door it says HOMEWRECKER.

The tears start falling before I even realize I am crying. My baby has been vandalized. My pride and joy that I have worked so hard for. Not just vandalized, no, this was a personal attack on me.

The word homewrecker points to one person.

Tyler.

But that would mean he knows where I am. Wiping my tears, I do a three-sixty, taking in my surroundings. Nothing stands out. I wish I knew what he drove. The reality is he could be in any of these parked cars.

I pull out my phone and call Brett. He answers just as I spot a piece of paper under the windshield. I pull it out.

"Hello?"

It's a note meant for me. I take a deep breath, reading the words on it. I read them once more before I completely breakdown.

"Finnley! Are you okay? Where are you?" Brett's voice practically vibrates through my cell phone.

"He... he..." I take a deep breath. "He destroyed my car."

"Where are you?"

"I just finished meeting with a medical group. I'm about an hour away from home."

"Where are you, Finnley?" Brett growls.

"Titusville."

Brett curses before speaking. "What did Tyler do to your car? Is the car safe to drive?"

I look my car over once again. The fact that he knows it was Tyler scares me.

"I think it is safe to drive. It looks like he only keyed it."

"That's not a good enough response. Look under the car, check the gas cap. Tires."

I let out a sad sigh. This is all so overwhelming, but I do as he says.

"I'm no detective, but everything seems okay."

"Finnley, I want you safe. This is not something to joke about."

"I'm not joking! I am fucking pissed. Onyx has been destroyed."

"You need to get in your car and lock the doors. Call the non-emergency line and get a deputy out there to take a report. Call me back as soon as you finish with the deputy."

Ugh. This puts a snag in my dinner plans with Violet. Is this what I get for using a dating app? No, that is silly. Millions of people use dating apps every day and find their happily ever after.

Me, on the other hand, I am not that lucky.

"Finnley, did you hear me?"

"Yeah, okay. I'll call."

"Call me as soon as you finish, unless you don't feel safe, then call nine-one-one, and then me. Understand?"

"Yeah, yeah, so bossy. But hey, at least you're not grumpy."

"Finnley," Brett warns.

I laugh because if not I will just start crying again. "Ah, there he is. Okay, bye."

I kill the call before he can respond with some other stern warning because in typical Brett fashion, that is how he operates.

Just like Brett told me to do, I put in a call to the Titusville police department and wait for them to arrive.

I breathe out a sigh of relief as I turn onto Hawthorne Way. I am glad to be home. It took an officer about fifteen minutes to come out. He was amazing though and kept apologizing for getting held up on a previous call. He tried to reassure me that this type of thing happens often to women who leave a relationship.

It did nothing to reassure me. If anything, it has put me more on edge.

The only positive thing about getting home this late is that Brett will be getting off shift soon and he said he will be coming straight over. Which is fine with me. I'd rather not be alone tonight. I just hope he isn't expecting me to cook anything. Maybe I should text to grab some fast food on his way in even though I have no appetite. I'm still sick to my stomach over my car. Not to mention how much it will probably cost to have Onyx repainted. Poor thing. I have always taken such great care of my car. The shit that Tyler did to it really angers me.

I walk up the stairs to my apartment. Just as I go to stick my key in the lock, I hear my neighbor unlock her door. Within seconds, Ms. Pam has cracked open her door. She is a homebody and doesn't go out much. It's rare for her to be opening her door this late. Instantly, I turn to face her.

"Hey there, Finnley."

"Hi, Ms. Pam. Is everything okay?"

"Oh yes, my dear. I just wanted to let you know you had a few visitors today."

"Visitors? As in more than one?"

"Yes, at first there was this boy, well, I guess he isn't much of a boy. I wouldn't quite call him a man though, with the way he was pounding on your door."

I can feel the hair on my arms rise as a sick feeling begins to form in the pit of my stomach.

"Uh, I was not expecting anyone," I say because quite frankly, I don't know what else to say.

"I figured as much. He left after about ten minutes of pounding."

"What did he look like?"

Ms. Pam rubs her chin as she thinks over my question. "He was about average height. Brown hair, but not too dark. Not as dark as that handsome policeman you have over occasionally."

Woah. Ms. Pam is a nosy Nellie. Which really is not a big deal considering the fact that Tyler has light brown hair. His hair is much lighter than Brett's. That sick feeling only intensifies, causing me to shake my head.

"Everything all right, Finnley?"

"Yeah, I just was not expecting anyone today."

"I see. The other visitor looked like she could be your twin."

"My twin?!" I nearly gasp. There is no way in hell that my sister showed up here. No damn way.

"Oh yes, she looked very much like you. Her hair was shorter though."

For fuck's sake. Why on earth would Fia come by unannounced? I try to think back on the last time I saw my sister. It has been at least two years, I think.

Unlocking and pushing open my door, I nod to my neighbor. "Thanks for letting me know I had some people drop by."

She waves me on as she shuts her door, locking it right away. I do the same.

I toss my bag and keys on my kitchen counter and immediately head for the Malibu that is stored in the cabinet above the stove. Just as I pour some into a shot glass, someone pounds on my door, causing me to jump out of skin and drop the glass. Rum goes everywhere.

Just freaking great.

And such a shame that it has been wasted.

I rush over to my door because whoever is on the other side does not let up. I see that it is Brett. He's early.

I open the door and he storms in right away, slamming it shut behind him.

"I have been trying to reach you! Don't you look at your phone?" He is practically out of breath. If I was not worried before, I am now.

"I... my phone is on silent. I was talking to my neighbor."

"I told you to turn to ringer back on."

"Yeah, well, you know I don't listen." I shrug my shoulders and head back into my kitchen. I really need that damn drink.

Chapter Twenty-Eight

Brett

Finnley is going to be the death of me. I fucking swear. That mouth of hers. I have never wanted to shut someone up and kiss them at the same time. That was until she came into my life.

"You need to listen. It's for your safety."

"And your sanity," she states without looking back at me. I see the bottle of Malibu on the counter and can only assume she is making herself a drink. Rightfully so. I checked out her car before I rushed up to her apartment. My fucker of a brother did quite the job.

My blood starts to boil now that I know Finnley is safe in her apartment. The entire drive here I was in a panic because she wasn't answering my calls.

"Would you like half of a Malibu Bay Breeze?"

Finnley turns to me with a glass in her hand. A smile plastered on her face.

"What do you mean half?"

"Well, I'm out of pineapple juice, so it's just rum and cranberry juice."

I shake my head; she shrugs and takes a sip. I don't know how she does it. Somehow she eases the anger I feel. She makes me feel like I'm doing more than just existing. Like I'm starting to live again.

"I meant to text you to grab something to eat, but my neighbor stopped me."

"It's fine. How does pizza sound? I'll order us one."

"I don't care. I might not eat much so don't go crazy."

"Finnley," I warn. "You need to eat. We'll get your car fixed and get shit with Tyler handled."

"I think he stopped by today." The way she says it so casually I think I may have misheard her.

"I'm sorry, what?"

She takes a long sip of her half whatever. "My neighbor, she told me some guy stood at my door pounding on it for a little bit."

I wipe a hand down my face. "And? What else did she say?"

"That I had another visitor. My sister apparently. Said she looked just like me, but had shorter hair."

"You have a sister?"

"I do. We don't talk often because we don't get along. Complete opposites as my mother would say."

"Does your sister know Tyler?"

She laughs, her sexy little ass laughs. It both pisses me off and turns me on.

"Hell if I know. I mean, anything is possible, right? Look at me going on dates with your brother."

"Pack your things. We will hit a drive-thru on the way back to my place."

I pull out my phone, sending a quick text to update Scott and Luke, along with my lieutenant. Earlier today, I made them aware of the situation with Finnley and her car. I also reached out to the officer in Titusville. He is forwarding me over a copy of the police report.

"Brett, come on, you can't be serious."

"I. Am. Dead. Serious." I pronounce each word slowly. She needs to understand the severity of this situation. My brother knows what she drives. He knew where she was at today.

"Fine. But only until this gets sorted." She points between me and her. "We are not ready to reside together."

That stings. Not that I want Finnley to move in with me or anything like that. It's just how she said it. I also understand that she is not happy with said situation. She's probably going to hate me with what I am about to say.

"You are also going to leave your Camaro here. We'll get you a rental in the morning."

Just like I figured, she groans in frustration and storms off. I decide it is best to wait here in the kitchen. She could use some privacy while packing her things.

While waiting, I decide to put away the Malibu and wash the shot glass, her glass. I clean up what looks to be spilled rum too.

I don't want to rush her, but I'm growing impatient. What could she possibly be packing that is taking this long?

I walk down the hallway to her room. Her door is ajar and while I want to be respectful of her privacy, I walk in anyway.

I stop short when I see her. Her long red hair streams down her back as she zips up a piece of luggage. She hangs her head low and lets out a sad sigh.

I realize this must be hard for her. Her car has been vandalized. She is not safe in her apartment. It's only fair that she's struggling.

I also realize that I need to be the one to comfort her. To be the one she feels safe with. In order to do so, I need to open up. I must let her in.

"Finnley," I say quietly. "Can I help you with anything?"

She stands up straight. I love that she is a confident woman.

"I just finished. If you want to grab this, I just have a tote I need to grab from my car."

"Okay."

I take her luggage down and stop by her car to grab whatever she needs for work. She climbs into my cruiser and does not say a word.

Placing her things in the trunk, I think back to the last time she took a ride in my cruiser. She was shit faced drunk from being stood up. Fury starts to coarse through my veins as I remember that she was stood up. Everyone that worked there knew it too. I bet it was my brother that caused her to drink as much as she did.

That's a question for later. Right now the only thing I want to do is to get us both something to eat and to make sure she actually eats. Then the plan will be to get her settled and give her space until she wants comfort.

"Can we have sex tonight?"

"What?"

"Look, I've had a rough day. I just want a shower and to get lost in an orgasm. If you could fulfill that wish, that would be great."

Fuck if her words don't make my dick twitch. This woman is always surprising me. Always.

Chapter Twenty-Nine

Finnley

After taking the last bite of my dinner, I wipe my mouth with my napkin and place it on top of the box that my chicken sandwich came in. Brett demanded that I eat something. I did and now I am stuffed. I know he's in protective mode, worried about me and all that bullshit, but right now all I want to focus on sex. I want to get lost, to drown in the stars while he causes me to fall apart at his touch.

Yes, that is what I want.

I want it very much, and I want it right now.

The thoughts of what he can do to my body alone have me squeezing my thighs. There is no denying that I am wet either. The fact that he is still in uniform also does not hurt.

Standing, I grab my trash. Brett finished his dinner before me but has been glued to his phone.

I'm sure he is doing all sorts of police work. He certainly paid no attention to me wanting a shower and sex. Guess I need to remind him.

"I need to shower."

He nods but never takes his eyes off whatever it is he is looking at. So I do what I do best, I make him look.

I unbutton my navy dress pants. After shimming them past my hips and ass, I let them hit the floor. I do the same with the white thong. I very casually step out of them. Each step brings me one step closer to Brett's side of the table. I pull the white blouse over my head and drop it to join the other pieces of clothing that lay at my feet.

All that is left on me is a white lace, front clip bra. I won't lie, it is one of my favorites. It pushes up my boobs just right and unclasps with one hand. Sexy and convenient.

The second I do unclasp it, my boobs explode out of it. I slide the straps down and off before holding it in my hands.

This entire time Brett has not noticed me standing here. Not even now as I stand before him, completely naked.

I toss my bra at Brett. It practically lands in his hands, right on top of his cell phone. Without waiting to see his response, I turn and head for his room.

I want that shower, and I want him.

I have barely made it halfway down the hall when I hear the chair slide back. I smile.

Seconds later, Brett's hand snakes around my waist, halting me.

"Finnley," he whispers seductively in my ear.

The thrill of what his words do to me turns me on further. My nipples harden into pebbles.

"Brett," I reply, my words barely a whisper.

"You're teasing me."

"Not exactly, I did say I was going to shower."

"You threw your bra at me."

I turn my head to look at him. "I wanted to make sure you heard loud and clear that I was going to take a shower. Don't want you thinking that I disappeared."

Placing my hand over his, I slide it down my stomach until we reach my pussy. I then remove my hand from his. His hand stays in place while one of his fingers pushes through my soaked lips.

A growl leaves him mouth and for some reason that makes me giggle.

"What are you doing to me?" he asks as he thrusts another finger in.

Finally. He is touching me, helping me escape the current nightmare that is my life. My head falls back on his chest.

"What are you doing to me?" he repeats again, this time in my ear. He trails little kisses under my ear, along my jaw line.

If I didn't have goosebumps before, I most certainly do now.

"I told you I wanted sex and a shower."

"That you did," Brett says as he starts to walk us into the room. All the while his two fingers continue to tease me.

Only when we reach his bathroom does his hand leave my most sensitive part.

Brett steps around me and walks over to the shower and turns it on.

"Are you showering with me?" I ask.

Without replying, Brett grabs me by my hips and lifts me up onto the bathroom counter.

"I haven't decided yet."

I raise an eyebrow. "Oh really?"

The man that stands before me is no longer paying attention to me. Well, I mean he is paying attention to my body, but not my words.

His hands might still be on my hips, however, those baby blues are fixated on my bare pussy. Pure desire oozes with each breath he takes.

Watching him stare at me makes me feel like a goddess.

It also makes me that much hotter. Even though he just had his hands on me, I am still starving for his touch.

With Brett lost in a trance, I take the opportunity to do the same. I take him in from head to toe.

From his dark hair to the light stubble along his jaw line.

Brett is fucking gorgeous.

How his wife left him for his brother is beyond me. Tyler might be hot, but he is nothing compared to the man in uniform that stands in front of me.

I spot his erection through his cargo pants. I reach out and grab it.

Brett's eyes finally shoot up to mine. He looks like he wants to scold me.

"Don't look at me like that. Not unless you plan to bend me over this counter to fuck me."

He opens his mouth to say something, but no words come out. I've surprised him.

"That's what I thought, now undress. I need you to fuck me now."

The Adam's apple on his neck bobs as he nods his head. He does as I say though, and strips out of his uniform.

Then he finally fucks me into oblivion.

Chapter Thirty

Finnley

I take a sip of my coffee while replaying all the things Brett did to my body last night. Gentle yet strong hands roamed my body, teased my body. His tongue licked, sucked, nibbled my most sensitive areas. His mouth did unspeakable things to me. Things that would make most blush. Not me though. I welcomed the things he did with open arms.

He left early this morning in Onyx. He said he was dropping it off at an auto body shop. Something about knowing the owner. It was hard to hand over the keys. I have never let anyone drive my car. That Camero is my baby. He did offer to drive me to get a rental, but I knew he also had to be at work, so I declined. Him taking my car to the shop is more than enough.

As soon as my phone dings, I see it is the Uber

driver to take me to pick up my rental. I set my mug in the kitchen sink and toss my handbag over my shoulder before heading out.

A gray four-door sedan is what I am looking for. As soon as my feet hit the bottom of the stairway, I spot the car.

"Hey, thanks for the ride," I say casually as I climb in the back seat. The driver who is wearing a black ball cap and sunglasses gives me a nod before putting the car and drive. As the car accelerates, the doors lock. A typical feature with many cars. One that makes me feel safer.

I lean back and scroll aimlessly on social media while the driver takes me to my destination. That is until the driver clears his throat.

"Hello, Finnley." That voice instantly causes a sick feeling to in my stomach.

Tyler.

My head snaps up as I nearly drop my phone in my lap.

"Don't look so surprised to see me."

"Wha... how?" I whisper as straight fear begins to fill every single ounce of my being. I look up at his reflection in the review mirror.

"How am I? Is that what you are asking? Well, I was doing great until you started fucking around with my brother." Tyler's words are laced with straight venom. He's the snake and I, the unsuspecting prey.

When I don't reply, he continues.

"Tell me, why did you go for him? What drew you to Brett?"

I shake my head, not answering him. Why does he even want to know the answers?

"I asked a fucking question! I want answers."

I jump in the back seat at his raised voice. "I, I didn't know he was your brother." I do my best to swallow down any ounce of fear. The last thing he needs to know is that I fear him. "He was there the night you stood me up, so if you want to blame someone, blame yourself."

Throwing that in his face makes me feel good. Sadly, it is short lived and replaced with fear once again. Tyler all but growls while jerking the steering wheel. He turns down a road I am not familiar with and floors it.

My flight or fight response kicks in. I yank on the door handle. It's locked. Of course it fucking is. I heard the lock when the car got up to speed. My cell phone sits on my lap. I am not sure if he knows that, and I sure don't want him to know that. I casually grab my handbag from the seat next to me, and put it on my lap, clutching it like a scared child. Hell, I am scared. I need to keep him distracted so that I can try to text or call Brett for help.

"How did you know I was leaving the house?" I ask as calmly as possible.

"That was easy. I've been watching you. I saw

my dickhead of a brother leave with your car. I knew it was a matter of time before he returned or that you would order a ride. Just as I was about to give up, I saw a car pull up that I didn't recognize. I walked up and asked the poor guy if he was there for you. When he said yes, I yanked him out and threw his ass in the trunk."

"What?!" I turn back and look at the trunk in complete disbelief. "Is he, is he okay?"

"Should be." Tyler shrugs his shoulders as if he doesn't give the slightest fuck that he just carjacked someone and that they are currently in trunk.

Feeling my phone in my hand, I know I need to get it unlocked in order to call for help.

Facial recognition.

I slide the tan handbag forward slightly and swipe up on my phone. Leaning forward I try to make sure my face matches up.

"Hey, don't be getting sick on me. I don't have time for that shit."

Awesome, he thinks I am nauseous. I lean forward a little more. It's just enough for the phone to register and unlock.

Thank God.

I stay leaning forward, pretending to breathe heavily. I should just call 911 but I know I would only have seconds to speak before Tyler cut me off. Instead, I text Brett.

`He has me.`

Within seconds my phone starts ringing. Fuck. I sit up and look at Tyler through the review.

"Who is that?"

I glance down and back up. "Brett. He probably wants to know if my Uber driver has picked me up." I shrug in an effort to play it cool.

The phone stops ringing and starts back up.

Tyler hits his hand on the steering wheel. "Answer. Tell him you got picked up and end the call. I don't need him blowing up your phone."

With shaking hands, I pick up my phone and hold it to my ear.

"Hello."

"Listen to me carefully, just answer yes or no. Say nothing else. Tyler, has you?"

"Yes."

Do you feel safe?

"No."

"Do you know where he is taking you?"

"No." My voice cracks as reality washes over me. I don't know where he is taking me. Or what the hell his plans are.

"Finnley, what does he want? End the call now." Tyler attempts to whisper except it comes out sounding more like a growl.

"That fucker. Is your location on?"

"I think so. I'll check when I get back." I throw a wink at Tyler hoping to satisfy him. It doesn't work. He all but slams on the breaks. I nearly lose my grip on my phone.

"Jesus!" I shout at Tyler.

"Finnley!"

Tyler turns into some plaza. It looks abandoned. Totally not a place I would want to come.

"I think my car is ready," I say into the phone. It's a wasted effort, but I try anyway.

"Act like you are hanging up, and keep the line open. Put your phone in your pocket. Do you understand?"

"Okay. Bye."

I pretend to hang up and slide my phone into my bag, zipping it close.

Tyler is cursing to himself as we pull up and park in front of a building. There are no signs to tell me anything. There's one white car parked a few spots down.

He kills the engine and turns in a haste in his seat to face me. He pulls out a knife and points it at me. I sit back as far as the back seat will allow. I suddenly wish I was in the trunk with the poor Uber driver, who I sure hope is okay.

"Don't try no bullshit. No running. I won't hesitate to hurt you."

I nod. There is not a doubt in my mind that he

will do just that. In fact, I am certain he does plan to harm me in some shape or form.

He gets out and comes around to my side. When he opens the door and grabs my arm, I try to throw the strap of my handbag over my head. He is quick though and grabs my hand, preventing me from doing so.

"You won't be needing that purse. Out. Now"

I swallow. I hope whatever Brett needed to be able to track me, he got.

I must hold on to that hope. It's all I have at this point.

Tyler has a strong grip on my upper arm, and the knife is visible in his other hand. I could possibly try to fight him to get away. But that all changes the second a door opens and out steps Fia.

My sister.

My fucking sister.

Chapter Thirty-One

Finnley

How on earth does Fia know Tyler? How does Tyler know Fia? The questions run through my mind along with the fear. Side by side.

"Hello, Finn, it's been a while," Fia says. Her voice is wispy-like, the voice of an angel as my mother used to say. I used to be jealous of how sweet she sounded. Now, it only makes me cringe. Gone are the days when we got along.

My sister changed after our mother died, and we haven't seen eye to eye since. We hardly talk, and to be quite frank, I prefer it that way.

Fia has always been, what's the word... selfish. Life was always about her. My mother played a part in her being the way she is. She would enable her, so to speak. Fia was older. I was the baby. I know many say the baby of the family is the one that gets spoiled, but not in my case. My mother doted on Fia daily. While she loved me, I think she loved Fia more. When our mother passed away from cancer, there was no one to continue the enabling, the spoiling. I certainly did not condone her selfish ways and so I became the enemy.

Closing my eyes, I reimagine the last time I spoke to my sister. She dropped by my place unannounced. I invited her in, only for her to start making demands that I pay for things for her. I remember leaning against the kitchen counter asking her what she did with her inheritance. It wasn't a monstrous amount. But enough that she could live comfortably. For a long time.

Me, I received some of my mom's fine china. Whatever, I didn't hold it against Fia because well, my mother was the one responsible, and she was no longer alive.

I take a deep breath. That night, Fia became very angry. She was livid over the fact that I would not financially support her. When I asked her to leave, she passed by the shelf that held all of the fine china and proceeded to swipe her hand, row by row. Shattering the only things that I inherited.

From that day forward, I vowed that I would never be disrespected in such a way ever again.

And I wasn't until now.

My short trip down memory lane comes to an abrupt end when my sister slaps me across the face.

I can't even grab my face to rub the tender spot because Tyler is still holding my arm.

"What the hell was that for?"

"You still think you are too good to speak to me. Miss High and Mighty." She laughs, almost sinister. So much for angelic. "We will just have to take you down a notch or two." Fia winks at me while holding the door to this unnamed building open. Tyler forces me to walk inside. I hear the door slam shut behind me.

The room is dim. It smells musty as if it has been vacant a long time. It probably has been.

"Where do we want her?" Tyler asks.

Fia walks past us and opens a door on the right. "In here is fine for all I care." She continues down the hall and disappears.

Tyler forces me into the room. He keeps a tight grip on me. Four bare walls. There are no windows. No way to escape. I keep my fear in check by reminding myself that I am a strong confident woman.

Holding my head high, I ask, "Why did you bring me here?"

Tyler lets out a sarcastic laugh, not bothering to answer my question.

"Is it another date you want?" I know it probably isn't wise to poke the bear. I do it anyway.

"Shut the fuck up, you little cunt." Tyler brings the knife up to my throat.

All confidence I felt seconds before has left my body. Replaced with straight fear for my life. What is he capable of? I have no idea. My heart rate picks up along with my breathing. I feel the tears threatening to spill. He sees them, too, and smiles.

"Good. You should be afraid." Tyler leans in close. "You should fear me because I am nothing like my brother.

He sure as hell isn't. Taking a deep breath, I try to calm my nerves. It's useless.

"How do you know my sister?" I ask in attempt to piece this disaster of a puzzle together.

"Your sister and I met through Brett's wife. They used to work together." He smirks. "Fia and I have kept in contact, meeting up occasionally. Your last names were the same so I asked her if you two were related. Fia was more than happy to help me with my quest."

A shiver runs down my spine. "Where is Brett's ex-wife?"

Tyler shrugs like he has zero cares in the world, and maybe he doesn't. "She took off. I couldn't give her all the things she longed for. As much as she loved me, I didn't hold all the bells and whistles that my fucking brother did."

Interesting, considering he didn't kidnap her in the same way that he has me right now. Hell, maybe he did. There is no telling.

"What do you want from me?"

"I wanted a chance. A decent fucking chance. But no, you had to go a fuck my brother. He's always tried to take what is mine. I lost one woman because of him. I'm not losing another." His words are laced with hate. Pure hate.

"I already told you that I didn't know you two were brothers."

"Oh please," Fia says casually as she walks into the room. My eyes fly to her hands. It looks like she is holding zip ties, and I can't quite make out what the other thing is. "They look alike. They are brothers, after all."

I squint, while studying Tyler's features. Now that I am paying attention, I can see the resemblance. Same prominent Jaw line. Same blue eyes. Brett's hair is obviously darker. Even still, I had no idea.

"I honestly had no idea." I look at Tyler. "If you hadn't stood me up, I would never have gone out with Brett."

Tyler's hand connects with my cheek so fast that it stuns me. The force causes me to stumble backward.

I was not expecting Tyler to haul off and slap me. I mean, I guess I should have with my smart mouth and all. But fuck, it hurts. Fia laughs as she comes up behind me. She rubs my cheek the same way a mother would rub her child's cheek.

"If you weren't such a bitch you wouldn't be in

this predicament." She moves behind me as she grabs my arm, yanking it behind me. She chuckles. "Maybe this will teach you that it doesn't pay to be so perfect, so righteous. All I wanted was a chance to be your sister, your friend. But no."

"Ouch! What the fuck?"

I want to fight her off. I really do, yet Tyler stands before me, knife still in hand, twirling it while watching us with wild eyes.

"Just because I didn't feed into your habits the same way our mother did doesn't mean I was being a bitch. I was being real. Why can't you see that?"

"Stupid, Finnley. So stupid," my sister says as she shoves me back toward a corner, causing me to fall on my ass with no way to break my fall. It hurts like hell too. I end up biting my tongue from the impact. I can already taste the blood as my eyes begin to water.

Fia turns to Tyler. "You can play with her first. Do whatever. Just keep her alive so that I can have my fun too." She glances at me and winks before walking out of the room.

I try to pull my arms apart from one another, but it is useless. The plastic digs into my wrists so damn hard.

Tyler continues twirling the knife with his hand while staring at me. Well, staring at my body. His eyes skim over me from head to toe. It makes me feel gross.

He must notice my disgust because he kneels in front of me and laughs.

"Look at you, all worried." He reaches out and pets me like I am a dog. "Don't move an inch otherwise you'll bleed. We don't want to make Fia mad, okay?"

I stay completely still. I don't even nod yes or no. Instead, I practically hold my breath.

He flicks the knife in his hand and brings it up to my collarbone. In one swift move, he slices my shirt from the neckline all the way down to my waist. Sliced it right open. He pushes open my shirt, exposing my black bra.

Tyler's eyes light up. He takes the knife and taps me once on each breast. He lays the knife between them and moves his hands to my yoga pants. Yanking them straight down. My pussy is now on total display for his grimy ass. I curse myself for not wearing at least a thong. What I would give to be able to cover myself up. My stomach starts to churn.

"I'm going to enjoy this."

"Why are you doing this?" I ask again as the tears start to really fall. The thoughts of what he can and will probably do to me is too much.

"Because I can," he states as he picks the knife back up and traces it down my stomach. He applies pressure, it fucking stings.

Tyler holds the knife up to me. The slightest

bit of red is on the tip. He takes the knife to his mouth and licks it.

I squeeze my eyes shut. I don't want to see anymore. I can't.

Little by little Tyler is stripping away the woman I am. He is going to destroy me. I just know it.

Chapter Thirty-Two

Brett

"For fuck's sake!" Why isn't my cruiser going faster? The pedal is to the metal, yet it feels like I'm moving in slow motion. I swear if something happens to Finnley, I will not forgive myself. And Tyler, well, he is a dead man either way. What the fuck is wrong with my brother?

He already got my wife. Was Abigail not good enough? Now he has the first person who has breathed life back into me. The woman who managed to break down the walls made of stone. The walls I put up to protect myself from any devastation ever again.

Five miles away. According to the coordinates on Finnley's phone. I had it pinged immediately. Her location has not moved in over ten minutes. That is if her phone is still on her. It's been quiet on the line for a while now and that alone is making me fucking anxious.

God, I sure fucking hope her phone is still on her. Otherwise, I don't know what I'll do.

You'll fucking kill him.

That is exactly what I will do. No doubt about it.

Luke comes over the radio, telling me he will most likely arrive before me. Back up is in route.

"Copy," is all I say. I want to say more, so much more. Like don't fucking kill him. Leave that part for me. However, that sort of talk would be frowned upon. It's best to say nothing

I check the coordinates again.

Four miles.

When Finnley texted me those three words, I almost lost it. I should not have left her alone. Not for one fucking second. I try to tell myself that I wouldn't have if I truly knew what my dumbass of a brother was capable of.

Fucking Tyler. When I get my hands on him, he will regret ever fucking with her. With me. I'll make sure of it.

Three miles.

"Just pulled in. Two cars in the plaza."

"Almost there."

Knowing that Luke is there should bring my anger down a notch.

It doesn't.

Two miles.

I hope like hell she is where her phone last pinged because if not, I will search high and low until I find her. What if I don't find her? What if Tyler does the unspeakable? My thoughts take a dark turn and with that dark turn, the rage I feel only intensifies.

One mile.

Tyler wanted to date Finnley. They went on a few dates from what I understand. If he touches her, so help me. I'll cut off his fingers one by one. I'll cut him inch by inch.

I let off the gas as I come up on the plaza. It's an old plaza that has seen better days. Overgrown shrubs outline the perimeter. There is a giant for sale sign just before the entrance. A desperate attempt to breathe this place back to life.

There are already three other officers here. At least from what I can see.

I hope they have Finnley.

I hope they have Tyler.

I don't even bother pulling into a parking spot. I throw my cruiser in park directly behind the gray car. It is the exact pinged location as Finnley's phone.

Fear fills me. What if her phone was left behind?

I shake my head. There's no time to think like that. Not right now.

Jumping out, my hand is already on my holster, removing my gun. I shut the door quietly while looking around.

There are no other officers out here. That means they must be in one of the four units.

Fuck.

How come no one has come on the radio yet? I walk up to the gray car. No one is in it, but I peer inside anyway. When I see Finnley's purse, my heart sinks.

I all but run up to the unit that is to the left of the gray car. The door is locked. Where the fuck is everyone?

I radio Luke as I head for the next unit. I hear what sounds like muffled cries. I stop dead in my tracks and listen.

My eyes fly to the trunk of the car as an unmarked deputy pulls in. I run back to the car, yank the door open and hit the button for the trunk.

By the time I rush to the back of the car, the other deputy is rushing up.

"Holy shit!" he shouts.

I'm stunned too. There is a guy in the trunk. He's crying.

"Where is she?" I question even though I am already certain he has no damn clue.

The guy shakes his head, snot and tears flying. He is visibly shaking.

"I... I... he knocked me out." The poor guy is a damn mess. He can't even talk straight.

"We need an ambulance," I say into my radio.

"What happened?" the other deputy asks.

Thank fuck he asks because I have already started jogging away, heading to the next unit.

Just as I approach the second unit with my gun drawn, the door flies open. A woman runs out of the door. How many fucking people has my brother kidnapped? Before I can speculate too much, Luke flies out after her. He practically tackles her to the pavement.

What in fuck?

The woman's face hits the ground, and she screams out in pain. She starts to wiggle and put up a fight. I run over and help secure the woman. She has red hair like Finnley. How fucking strange.

It doesn't take long for us to get her cuffed. Luke sits her up and shoves me back.

"Go, she's in there." He nods to the unit he just chased this chick out of. Then he gets on his radio and requests another ambulance.

I am frozen in place. My fucking heart sinks.

"Is she— "

"Fucking go in there, Hayworth!" Luke all but shouts at me.

As soon as I step over the threshold, the odor hits me. It is stale. I've smelled worse though.

"Finnley!" I shout as I come up to a room on

the right. In the hallway just up a bit from the door the two other officers. They have their guns aimed at my brother. His tan shirt has blood on it. It better be his fucking blood.

I'll admit, the sight makes me pause, and I nearly have to catch my breath. Never in a million fucking years would I have envisioned my brother surrounded by cops with their guns aimed at his head.

Tyler spots me and smiles. The fucker has the audacity to smile at me after kidnapping my girl.

My girl.

"Brother," he says sarcastically, while a little blood spills from his mouth, and he winces. "It has been a while. I hope you like what I've done to that whore of yours."

All the rage that has been locked tight explodes. I lunge at him, shoving one of the officers out of my way. We both fall to the ground. Tyler attempts to fight me off, but he seems weak. Me, what do I do? I hold a gun to his head while I wrap my free hand around his throat and squeeze.

"You piece of shit!" I yell while continuing to squeeze. The fucker attempts to laugh in my face. He barely puts up a fight which surprises me.

What happens next, I'm not sure. Someone grabs my gun from my hand before grabbing me, pulling me off of him.

"Get it together Hayworth! Now!" Luke slaps

my chest. "She fucking needs you. Let us deal with him."

I jerk free from his grip and run my hands through my hair. When I look up, I see it. The sorrow in his eyes. He steps back and shakes his head. I can hear the ambulance in the distance.

"She's in that room. Try to keep it together."

I swallow the fear of what I am about to find.

Very slowly, I push open the door that was half-closed. All the air leaves my lungs at the sight in front of me. There in the corner is Finnley, rocking back and forth. Her head is cast down.

I force my feet to move, dropping to my knees in front of her. She is naked from the waist down, that much I can tell. Her knees are pulled up to her chest.

"Finnley."

No other words come out. There are no fucking words. I can smell blood. That makes me worry. I'm hoping like hell it is just Tyler's blood that I'm smelling.

The woman in front of me jolts her head up at my words. Wide eyes that are bloodshot and filled with tears stare back at me. I want to reach out and touch her. So fucking badly. Unfortunately, years of training have taught me to do otherwise. Especially not knowing what my brother has done.

Instead I ask, "Are you hurt? Did he touch you?"

Finnley sits up a little straighter and holds her head higher. My eyes never leave hers. Not once.

She lifts her hands and pulls apart her top, revealing just what Tyler has done.

All the air leaves my lungs as I roll back off my knees.

He marked her body. With what, I am not one hundred percent. If I had to take a wild guess I would say some sort of knife. Lines upon lines mar her delicate skin. Her pale skin is stained with red.

My emotions get the best of me, and I lose it. I fucking lose it. Tears fill my eyes. The rage I felt was nothing compared to what I feel now.

"He's dead. He's so fucking dead." Instantly I stand up.

"Don't leave me! You can't leave me." Finnley's broken words freeze me in place. Taking a deep breath, I will myself to calm down. I have to.

"Brett, don't leave me."

I nod and squat back down.

Finnley needs me. She needs me now more than ever. And like she breathed life back into me when I was at my lowest, I know I need to man up and do the same. Even as the rage flows through my veins, I need to focus on her.

I search her sad eyes. She's been crying, no doubt about that. I can't begin to imagine the pain she is in. There is one question that does need to be asked. One that cannot wait. I hate that I even have to ask it.

I lean into her ear so that only she can hear me. "Finnley, did he..." I swallow thickly in order to force the words out of my mouth. "Did Tyler rape you, or sexually assault you in any way?"

Her entire body begins to tremble. Tears stream down her face. I swear, I might fucking lose it.

"Finnley, talk to me," I say as I grind my teeth together to keep from losing my shit. My patience is long gone.

"Hayworth, a word," Luke says from behind me.

"Not now." I don't bother turning to look at him, my eyes are focused on one person. The fiery red head who came barreling into my life with a mouth full of sass sits before me, beaten and broken.

"Hayworth."

This time I turn and stare down my co-worker and friend. He nods at Finnley once before tilting his head for me to follow. Whatever he has to say better be good.

I start to walk toward him.

"You can't leave me!" Finnley's frantic cries silence the room we are in.

I rush back to her along with Luke. He puts a hand on my shoulder.

"Finnley, we are not leaving this room. I am just going to speak to Brett right over there."

Luke points to the corner opposite of where she is. I really want to deck him. Clearly, she is not okay.

However, Finnley surprises me by nodding at him. "Yeah, okay, that is okay."

Luke chuckles as he pats my chest, giving me a slight shove to follow him. This time when I do, she does not scream or panic. Her tears have even slowed. I notice a white blanket in his hand.

"What?" I snap.

"We already have a statement from her. She told me everything. At least I think everything. She said he only ripped her clothes off her and fondled her breasts."

Rage fucking pours from every ounce of me. At this point, I do not care if I end up in prison. I look over at her. Her eyes are already on me. I try to give a slight smile to reassure her that I am here and will not be leaving her side.

"Look, she needs to get checked out. Mention it to the medics to have her checked." He pauses not wanting to finish what I already know. "Just in case she is in shock."

I nod. My eyes never leave hers. Her usual bright emeralds have been dimmed, and I do not like it. In fact, I fucking hate it.

"Is he going to live?" Finnley asks, her voice nearly cracking.

"Who?"

Luke stays quiet, his face void of any emotion. Not really a surprise. Comes with the career.

"Tyler." Finnley's voice breaks.

Tilting my head I look at him for answers. He doesn't seem to want to give me any.

"Luke."

"She stabbed him in the lower abdomen." He glances past me to her.

He pats me on the chest, handing the blanket over. He walks out, leaving the two of us alone again. I walk back over to her while trying to read her face. It is unreadable aside from the obvious. She stabbed Tyler. That means she fought back. Good. That also means that he was already stabbed when I attacked him. Fuck him. I feel zero sympathy for him.

Luke is right though, she needs to be taken to the hospital. I am not focusing on that piece of shit.

"You need to go to the hospital. Get all of this cleaned up. You should not be worried about that monster."

She closes her eyes while nodding at me. I can tell she is not ready for all this. Unfortunately, she does not have much of a choice.

"Can I touch you?" I ask quietly, not wanting to upset her more.

She nods again and that is good enough for me. Considering the marks across her body, I gently lift her into my arms. I carry her out of that musty smelling building and to the awaiting ambulance. I have a thousand questions that I still want to ask her. I don't though. For the time being, I will just bite my tongue.

Chapter Thirty-Three

Brett

I used to think that losing Abigail to my brother was the worst thing to ever happen to me. Almost losing Finnley to my brother, that is worse.

Way fucking worse.

My stomach is still in knots. Having to hear her replay the events to the caseworker at the hospital nearly gutted me. I even tried to step out of the room to give the two of them privacy when I couldn't stand another minute, but that caused Finnley to have a full on panic attack. So I stayed.

I haven't left her since.

Not even now that we are back at my house. She is currently crawled up on my couch, clutching one of those decorative pillows.

Sighing, I open my phone to see if there are any updates on Tyler.

Last I was told, he was still critical. Something about blood loss. I couldn't care less though. I realize that might make me a heartless son of bitch to some, however, it would not be further from the truth. Just staring at Finnley while she rests reminds me that I am more than just existing.

I care about her. More so than I ever cared about Abigail. The realization was a bitter pill to swallow last night. It's a different type of love than what I felt with Abigail. It was hard to admit to myself that I love Finnley. To care about her in such a way.

I'm not sure if these feelings stem from the fact that my own brother, my flesh and blood, attacked her in such a violent way or if it is because I have finally let her in all the way.

Regardless, I love Finnley Thompson.

And she is going to know it.

Finnley starts to stir, pulling me from my thoughts.

Finally.

I walk over and sit on the coffee table. There is a good chance she will freak out when she wakes up. I need to make sure I'm the first thing she sees.

We got home late last night, and she passed out on the way home. I had planned to run her a bath, but she was dead weight when I carried her in. I figured it was better to let her sleep than to wake her. I did not want to leave her to sleep in some hospital-issued gown and throw away undergarments. But waking her after she crashed from all the amount of trauma and shock wasn't an option.

Her eyes flutter open before she sits up fast. She raises her hand as if she is ready to hit me.

Flight or fight.

"Easy, Finnley. It's me, it's Brett," I say quietly and make no movement.

Her eyes are wild as she stares at me. She debates for a split second before lowering her hand down.

"Good morning, well, afternoon. It is after two," I say with a slight smile.

Her eyes don't leave mine. While I can't be certain, I'd say she is replaying yesterday's events in her head.

And I fucking hate that.

"Finnley, I am going to run you a bath. Will that be okay?"

She looks down and touches the gown that she left the hospital in before looking back up at me. She nods and stands like she is on autopilot.

She is just going through the motions.

I don't like it. Not one damn bit.

I reach my hand out for her to take, and like the fiery woman she is, she walks past me.

When she walks into my bathroom, she does not head for my tub. Instead, she walks straight for the shower and turns it on.

"I thought I would run you a bath," I say as I stand in the doorway.

"Right now, I just want to rinse all of this away." She holds open her gown, revealing lines of dried blood.

The anger that I have bottled away over the past several hours immediately starts to surface. Seeing her skin and now knowing exactly what he did, details and all. Her marred her. For life.

It infuriates me.

And while I would love nothing more than to let that anger out, I know I need to remain calm.

For her.

I nod. "I'll get you a washcloth."

Grabbing one from the cabinet, I bring it back to her. She is already in the shower. The gown she was wearing is now on the floor. I pick it up and toss it in the wastebasket. She will not be needing that ever again.

When I peer in from the entrance of my walk-in shower, the sight of her nearly takes my breath away. Finnley stands under the spray of water. She's not facing it, though. Instead, she is facing me. Water pours from above her, streaming down over her body. Her pale skin is red and angry. Her eyes are squeezed tight as if she is in pain. She must be in pain.

Even in pain, Finnley is breathtakingly beautiful. I know I said I would never fall in love again, even promised myself I wouldn't. However, the woman who stands before me has taken a piece of my heart without even knowing it. Finnley does not demand anything of me. She does not need me to impress her. She is just there, waiting with open arms.

That's how I know what I am feeling is love. Raw and real.

With Abigail, it was never like this. I never felt this way. It was always materialistic, a surface type of love. Deep down it was empty and full of lies.

Finnley's eyes open as I lean in to hand her the gray cloth. She looks down briefly at my hand, then back up at me. Something flashes in her eyes.

"Aren't you getting in with me?"

I'm taken aback. She can't be serious? She was just assaulted, stripped down to her soul.

"Brett?"

Finnley is waiting for me to acknowledge her, to answer her question. How do I do so without upsetting her?

She takes a single step toward me. Instantly I put my hand out.

"Finnley." I run a hand through my hair. Fuck, how do I say this without sounding like an asshole? "I, I had planned on letting you soak in the tub." I nod my head toward the tub, the same one she once bathed me in.

"I told you I did not want to soak until I scrubbed all of this off."

"Okay, well, I can start getting the tub ready for you." I turn away before she can say anything more. I make it to the tub before I hear her clear her throat.

"Am I too ugly now?"

He words nearly gut me. I hang my head as I lean over the tub.

Letting out a deep sigh, I stand up and walk back, stepping into the shower fully clothed. I walk up to her and grab her by the chin, forcing her to look me straight in the eye.

"Don't you ever think that. You understand? You are the most beautiful woman I have ever laid eyes on. Do you hear me?"

Finnley just stares at me.

"Finnley, I mean it. You are beautiful. These marks," I point to her angry abdomen, "don't change how I feel about you. I'm sorry if I caused you to have any doubt."

I run my hands through her wet hair, pulling it back away from her face while she studies me. She's searching for the truth. I can practically feel it pouring off her. So, I do what any man with a brain would do. I pull her in and kiss her. I kiss her like she's never been kissed before. I will make sure she feels everything that I feel for her.

After a slight hesitation, she allows me to

deepen our kiss. How long we stand there kissing, I can't be sure, but when we finally break apart, we are both out of breath.

"Wow," she whispers as she touches her swollen lips.

Fuck if it doesn't turn me on. I refrain. I refuse to cause her anymore pain. At least for tonight. I take a step back, giving he some space.

Finnley notices and steps closer. Desire now written all over her face. This certainly took a turn I wasn't expecting.

"Finnley," I warn.

It doesn't deter her, only eggs her on. She takes another step forward, reaching out to grab the erection that is obvious through my sweats.

I hiss the minute her hands take hold. This cannot happen. Not like this. Not while everything is so fresh.

"Brett." Straight seduction rolls off her tongue. She taunts me with the way she says my name.

"We can't."

"Why not?"

"You just went through a traumatic event. You need to get cleaned up and then you need to sleep and heal."

"I'm a little banged up. I'm not broken."

I shake my head. She's right, she is not broken. I was the one who was broken. Little does she know that she has slowly been putting me back together piece by piece.

I step to the edge of the shower. "Correct, you are not broken. But this is not how I plan to fuck the woman that I am falling in love with. And when I do fuck you, Finnley, I am going to worship every inch of your body, so I want you healed."

Then I step out of the shower, leaving her to soak in my words.

I meant what I said. When I do claim her as mine once and for all. She's going to feel it.

Chapter Thirty-Four

Finnley

I'm left speechless. Not in a million years did I expect Brett to ever speak the word love out loud. Hell, I did not think it was even in his vocabulary.

Yet, here we are.

He is falling in love with me. He said the words out loud. To me.

Am I dreaming?

I'd pinch myself for good measure except there is no need to. The stinging pain coming from my abdomen reminds me that I am in fact awake alive and breathing, even though I just survived a real-life nightmare.

I let out a long sigh before giving myself a pep talk. I would love nothing more than to wash it all away. The blood, the tears. Tyler's salvia. He spit on me a total of five times. Each time he questioned why Brett and not him. I answered honestly, and in return, he punished me by spitting in my face.

I gather water in my mouth and swish it around. Tyler also forced me to kiss him while he held the knife to my side. Like our previous kiss, it made me nauseous. This time, acid burned in my throat.

I shake my head at the memory. I refuse to let what Tyler did to me ruin me. I am a strong woman. I will not allow it. I expect a breakdown here and there, but no, he does not get the pleasure of breaking me.

Grabbing Brett's body wash, I pop the cap and pour the clear liquid into the cloth that Brett brought me. A woodsy scent fills the air. I welcome it. It's refreshing and the complete opposite of what that vacant building smelled like.

As soon as I finishing washing the filth off of my body, exhaustion creeps back in. The nurses and even Brett told me to expect it.

"Hey, Brett," I call out while rinsing the conditioner out of my hair.

"Yeah."

"Can I take a raincheck on the bath?" I feel terrible knowing he has already started prepping for it. I just can't do it right now.

"Uh, yeah, of course. Everything okay?"

"I'm just tired. I want to be wrapped up in a fluffy towel and carried off to bed."

Less than a minute later, the man who once was a grumpy cop appears at the entrance of the shower. He stands there in a pair of gray sweats, towel in hand. He truly is good to me. He may not realize that, but I do.

I turn the dial and head for him. I give him my back and like the gentleman he is, he wraps the towel around me. I turn to him and smile.

"Thanks."

Brett nods and then goes about picking me up. He carries me to his king size bed effortlessly. The sheets have already been pulled back for me. As soon as he sets me down, he walks out of the room. He seems like he is on a mission, so I don't bother to question. Instead, I unwrap myself and toss the towel on the floor. Then I pull up the sheets and wait.

He returns with a bottle of water and some pills. I hesitate before taking them.

"I told the doctor I didn't want— "

"Tylenol. Extra strength. Just to help with the discomfort."

I nod, taking the pills. He was listening. I told the doctor that I would not be filling any script for pain pills. No way. The cuts are surface wounds. No stitches were needed. I am not about to take crap that I do not feel is necessary.

"Do you want one of my shirts?" he asks.

"Sure."

He grabs one and gently puts it on me. I have to bite my lip to keep from trying to seduce him again. I can't help it. He's hot and the way his arm muscles flex awakens all the things I need, yet should not want considering what I have been through.

"I am going to shower real fast. The house is locked. Alarm is on."

I hesitate for only a moment. I am safe here, with him. "Okay."

I startle when I feel a dip in the bed. My eyes shoot open. A hand brushes against my cheek. I can almost feel his breath.

"It's just me. Go back to sleep."

I slap his hand away. My heart races as I sit up and throw the sheets off me.

"Shit, Finnley, I'm sorry. I didn't mean to scare you." He leans away from me.

It takes a few seconds before reality registers.

Brett.

I am safe. Safe with Brett.

"I, I'm sorry. You scared me."

"Finnley." Brett's stern words vibrate throughout my bones. "Don't you dare say sorry. It is natural to be jumpy, on edge. I shouldn't have touched you. It's a habit."

"I don't want you to stop touching me." I pause. "Ever."

The man who was once so cold stares at me.

His eyes flicker back and forth as he tries to process my words.

I watch as he swallows thickly before trying to work through what he wants to say. His strong jaw flexes each time he opens his mouth. He's trying to tip-toe through whatever it is.

I laugh a little and shake my head.

"Brett, I am bruised, not broken. Just say whatever it is you want to say."

"Tomorrow, we will be packing your things. Your home is here now."

He looks directly at me. He's serious. I half-thought he was going to give me some spiel about the trauma I have been through and how I am going to process it in stages. Telling me that I will be moving in with him was not even on the radar.

The thought sort of excites me. It also concerns me. I don't want him to be put out. He doesn't have to do this just because his brother hurt me.

"That's extremely nice of you. You don't have to do this, though."

"It's not up for debate."

"Brett—"

"No, Finnley. I will not have you living alone. Not while your sister is out on bond. She knows where you live. Who knows what else she is capable of."

His words make me stop for a moment. Fia was arrested. "She was released?"

"Yes, Finnley. She is out, walking free right now."

I nod slowly, trying to contain the wave of fear threatening to overtake me.

Brett holds his hand out. "She was slapped with a charge of accessory to commit a crime and committed battery. Easy bond." Brett shakes his head, clearly frustrated over the entire situation. I am too. But that doesn't mean I need to move in with the man. He doesn't need to take pity on me.

"Okay, let's be real for a minute."

"Finnley," Brett cuts me off, "I am being real. I haven't felt this alive in a very long time. I want to do life with you. I want to come home to you each night, and it would make me feel a thousand times better knowing you are here."

I nod sleepily. I hear him. I do. Loud and clear. It's just a lot to take in and I'm tired. So, I tell him the one word that will put his mind at ease.

"Okay."

"Okay," he replies.

I lean over to him. He freezes. I place a quick kiss on his cheek and then I climb back under the sheets and close my eyes.

I need sleep and a lot of it.

Chapter Thirty-Five

Finnley

I slept on and off for the past three days, which isn't like me. I am not one to normally lay around, not unless I am under the weather. This, however, was different. It was as if I had no control when exhaustion took over. Brett assured me many times that it was normal. Even still, I didn't like it.

Today, I am out of bed, showered, and fully dressed. I have a lunch date with Violet. Brett was not thrilled about me going out so soon, but I told him it was what I wanted and that after lunch we could go by my apartment to pick up some stuff.

Speaking of Brett, he walks into his room, or is it our room? I'm not completely sure how this works. I have never lived with a man before.

He stops just in front of me. I watch him as he assesses me from head to toe. Such a cop thing.

But also a Brett thing.

"You look beautiful." He runs a hand through his short dark hair while his eyes continue to roam my body.

"Thank you."

Not gonna lie, I like how his words make me feel. After what I have been through, after seeing myself in the mirror, I needed those words.

When the wounds heal and scar over, Brett will still want me. I know that everything will be okay. I honestly do. The mirror that I stand in front of may try to confuse me now and then, but Brett's words will always win.

Why? Because his words speak nothing but the truth.

"Are you ready?"

'I am," I reply as I walk up to him. His eyes have yet to leave my body. When his eyes meet mine, I feel it. It causes me to catch my breath.

He's searching. Searching to make sure I am fine. And I am. He is the reason I am fine. He just doesn't realize it yet.

I smile at the man in front of me, hoping that it will ease his mind.

"Let's go before I try to convince you to stay home."

I giggle at his words "Not a chance, I need to get out of this house."

There's a twinkle in his eyes as he smirks at me. This is the man I've come to care about.

Love, this is love, I tell myself.

I have not said the words out loud. When I begin to think about us and what he said a few nights ago about falling in love with me, it makes me feel some sort of way. It's hard to explain. My heart rate spikes, I feel almost ecstatic. But most of all, I think I am falling in love with him too.

* * *

"Why do you own all of this?" Brett asks for the second time while he brings some of my clothes inside.

"Because I am a female. We like to shop." I do. I won't sugarcoat it. I am a firm believer that shopping is a form of therapy. I am all for it.

"Do you care if we lay these out in the spare room until we rearrange the closets because I have a suspicion you will need my entire closet?"

Brett's shaking his head at me, but humor plays on his face. It is a nice change to see him happy. I don't think I will ever grow tired of seeing him this way.

"That works. I can always put my seasonal stuff in the guest closet."

"Seasonal?" He pauses. "You know what, never mind, I don't want to know."

This time, it is me who is laughing. It feels good to feel this light. So much heavy shit has happened, and it feels nice to begin to move forward.

Brett's phone goes off. He sets my clothes down carefully and pulls it out of his back pocket. I watch as he reads whatever is on the screen. His face instantly changes. Gone is the happy and playful Brett. It has been replaced with a serious one.

He looks up from his phone and tries to clear his emotions from his face.

He fails.

Bad.

"What is it?" I ask immediately.

He shakes his head. I know that he is attempting to conceal whatever message he just received. That alone is concerning.

"Brett, if we are going to do this," I point between us, "you are going to have to be honest with me. We cannot work if there are secrets."

He slowly nods at my words. I'm glad because I want us to work. He understands what is at stake. We both do.

I give him a minute. I know this man needs to work through what he wants to say.

I watch his Adam's apple bob as he swallows thickly before he clears his throat.

"That was Luke. Tyler has taken a turn for the worse."

Oh.

"Why don't you go see him? I'll be okay here."

Even though Tyler violated me in ways that I would never wish on anyone, he is Brett's brother. At the end of the day, they are blood. I might hate Tyler with every ounce of my soul, but that does not mean Brett should. I have my own opinion on how I feel about hearing Tyler's update. However, I refuse to push it on Brett. Plus, I do not want that kind of guilt on my chest. No way.

"No."

"What if... what if something happens?" Like him dying? I don't say that last bit. The air between us does it for me.

Brett says nothing. His stare penetrates mine. He does not even blink. I worry that he might be going into shock, or maybe he is numb.

It's ironic how our situations have flipped. First, it was me in shock and numb. All because of the same person, too.

"Brett, I think you should go see him," I say as I put the pile of clothes in my hand down.

"No."

"I will be fine. I think you should go. You never know what can happen." I try to express the seriousness of his situation. His brother taking a turn for the worse means he could very well die. I might not care if he does, but surely Brett will feel some sort of way. I do my best to wipe any emotion from my face. If he suspects even an ounce of hurt, he will refuse to go.

Brett sets his pile down next to mine and then turns to look at me. I mouth the word "go" in a last-ditch effort to get him to go. As much as I do hate his brother, I think he should go.

"I am not leaving you." Brett's words are firm. He turns and walks out of the empty bedroom.

This conversation is over.

Chapter Thirty-Six

Brett

Fuck!

I feel like shit for leaving Finnley behind as I storm out of the room. I'm certain she tried to conceal her feelings as she spoke. Little does she know I've learned to read her. Her eyes gave her away. I can't exactly explain it, but it's as if her eyes dim when sadness consumes her. Whether she is sad over what I said or the situation in general, I am unsure. If I were her, I wouldn't be sad at all. I would be happy as fuck.

Like I am.

Does that make me an asshole?

Probably. Yet, I don't care. Tyler deserves whatever fate he is dealt.

I open the slider and step out onto the back deck. I inhale a deep breath. I need fresh air, and I need a damn minute to get my thoughts in check.

My brother suffered a lot of blood loss. Apparently, Finnley got him good when she stabbed him. He also developed an infection based on what Luke said. Honestly, the details have gone in one ear and out of the other. My attention and focus have been on Finnley, and only Finnley.

I look back toward the door, grateful that she has not followed me out here. I fear if she was to come out, she would convince me to go see my fucking brother.

My mind has been made up since the day he assaulted the woman I love.

He is dead to me.

Fucking dead.

Breathing or not, he is dead to me.

I have no fucking desire to visit him in the ICU. The only reason I am getting any sort of update is because a deputy must stay at Tyler's bedside twenty-four-seven. I haven't asked about him, yet the guys feel like I should know his status.

I take another deep breath. Finnley's words replay in my mind. She thinks I should go and see him. I know deep down her words come from a place of sincerity. That's just like her though. Always caring and being concerned.

Even when I don't deserve it.

Hell, she could hate me for what my brother did. But she doesn't. Instead, that gorgeous redhead is moving her belongings into my place. She's encouraging me to see the person who assaulted her. She's still a ray of sunshine even though a hurricane just plowed through our lives.

I love her.

I fucking love her.

It's as if my brain is just registering that word for the first time in my life. Hell, maybe it is.

She deserves to know how I feel. Fuck that. She will know and she needs to know right fucking now.

To hell with my brother.

I march back into the house and call out for her. She steps into the hallway, with a puzzled look on her face.

"Finnley." I grab her hand and pull her close. With my other hand, I tilt her chin to look up at me. "I love you."

She scrunches her face. "But your bro—" She attempts to question me, but I lean in and kiss her to silence it.

I kiss her with everything that I have in me. I need her to understand how much I love her. What words cannot convey, I hope my kiss will.

Her lips are puffy when we part, and I like that it was me who caused them to look like that.

"Brett," she whispers.

"I love you. I fucking love you," I repeat while holding her face.

Tears fill her emerald eyes as they light up. A smile slowly forms.

"I love you. I love all of you. Even when you are grumpy, I love you."

She barely gets that last word out because my lips land on hers again while my hand slides around to grab the back of her head.

I kiss her.

Hard.

I cannot explain this feeling I feel inside of me. I feel light, no longer carrying about the weight of what Abigail and Tyler did to me. I no longer care about the hurt they put me through because their actions brought me to her.

This time when we part, Finnley looks at me with a serious expression.

"You need to see your brother. Please don't let me be the reason you do not go."

Not this again.

"Finnley," I warn.

"Why, Brett? Why not?" There is nothing but sincerity in her question.

I hold up a finger. "Number one, Tyler kidnapped you. He fucking hijacked the Uber driver and kidnapped you both." I take a deep breath before holding up a second finger. "Number two, he assaulted you. He marred your skin, your body, Finnley!" I'm not sure where the anger is coming from considering moments ago, I was elated. I try to swallow it down. For her sake. When I raise another finger, I see the first tear fall. "And number three, my asshole brother was having an affair with my wife. Fucking her in my home. He had no remorse for his actions. I did so much for him, and he fucked me."

"You're right. I'm sorry, Brett. I just, I did not want to be the reason you stay back and then come to regret it later."

Finnley's tears fall freely now, and it makes me feel like absolute shit. Gripping her chin, I force her to meet my eyes.

"I would never blame you. I cut Tyler out several years ago after what he did to me. You just happened to appear in the middle of it, and for that, I am sorry. I am so sorry he hurt you because of me. I am sorry you became a pawn in his sick game. I will spend the rest of my life making it up to you."

She nods, understanding my words. I gave her the truth. The brutal truth.

"What if he dies? Will I be blamed for his death?"

"Not a chance in hell, baby."

Finnley's eyes go wide. I've never called her that before. It just slid off my tongue ever so smoothly. Truth be told, I like how I sounded when I said it. What I like even more though is the way her face lit up when I said it.

"What now?" she asks.

"We rest. Let's go to bed."

Finnley nods as a sinister smirk forms on her lips.

"What?" I ask, curiosity getting the best of me.

Her cheeks turn a shade of pink before she looks me dead in the eye. "Make love to me tonight."

Her words cause my dick to stir, and I don't like it. She has to be kidding, yet her words are serious. There is no way.

"Finnley," I go to warn but she puts a finger on my lips, silencing me.

"I need this, Brett. More than you will ever know. I need you to touch me and erase the way he touched me."

I get her logic, but she isn't ready. Everything is still so fresh. The trauma, the words.

"No."

"Brett."

I shake my head while her eyes plead with me. I fucking don't like it. As much as my dick is straining and begging, I cannot go through with her request. Finnley needs to heal. She needs time.

Before I can rattle off all the reasons why it is a bad idea, my phone goes off. Another text message. I choose to ignore it, but less than a minute later my phone starts ringing. I hesitate before pulling out my phone.

"Answer it." Finnley nudges me.

I nod and pull out my phone just in time for me to miss the call. It was Luke.

The notification that appears at the top of the screen tells me all I need to know about why Luke called back.

My phone starts ringing again. I don't bother to answer it though. I keep rereading the text.

Tyler is dead.

Chapter Thirty-Seven

Brett

I stand there in complete silence while I read the text over and over. My phone starts ringing for the third time, or is it the fourth? I can't be sure. It is as if time has suddenly slowed.

"Brett." Finnley shakes me. "Brett, what is wrong?!"

I hear her words, yet they seem muffled, like I'm underwater. There is more ringing.

This time, Finnley takes the phone from me, and I let her.

I don't bother listening to the conversation. There is no point. My brother is dead. Nothing can be said to change that fact.

Finnley starts crying and rushes over to the couch to sit down. How ironic that she is the one breaking down. It makes no sense. The man did unspeakable things to her, and yet here she is crying over his death.

It takes me less than five minutes to allow this new reality to sink in before I shake my head. My number one concern is Finnley. I sit down next to her. I pull her in and push her messy red curls out of her face.

"Shh," I say while rubbing her back.

She sniffles. "I'm sorry, Brett. I mean, I am not sorry for stabbing him. He deserved it. I am only sorry that you lost your brother."

Just when I think this woman couldn't surprise me more when she speaks, she does. I think about her words. Relief floods me. She doesn't regret defending herself. No signs of guilt. I hope she never feels it.

As for my brother, I feel nothing. If I'm being honest with myself, the brother I once knew died a long time ago. He's been dead to me since before Finnley came barreling into my life. He played a stupid game and the end result cost him his life. Oh fucking well. It is one of those fuck around and find out situations. He fucked around, assaulted Finnley, and then found out what my girl was capable of.

My girl.

Pride suddenly fills in my chest. She is stronger than I have been giving her credit for. So much stronger.

I lean down and plant a kiss on her lips. My tongue darts out and I taste the salt from her tears. I lean back, my thumb swipes her cheek.

"Don't cry, baby."

Finnley shakes her head. "But... but he is dead. I killed him."

"Finnley," I say sternly while tilting her chin up at me. "You defended yourself. He kidnapped you, attacked you, violated you. He deserved his fate. You did nothing wrong. Nothing at all. Do you understand that?"

When she doesn't respond, I clear my throat to make sure she heard what I said. Her glossy eyes glance at mine before they cast down.

"Finnley," I all but growl.

There is no fucking way I will allow her to feel guilty about this. No fucking way.

"I need you to understand that you are not at fault."

"I killed a person..." She trails off, shaking her head.

I try hard to swallow down my frustration. It is the last thing she needs from me

"You killed a monster."

Silence hangs between us for less than a minute before I grow impatient.

"Do you hear me?"

This time she nods. She nods and looks up at me.

"I hear you, I do. It is just a lot to take in. I caused his death."

"Actually, an infection set in and let me remind you, he caused his death."

I rub my hands down Finnley's arms and lean down to kiss her cheek. I kiss her jawline, making my way to her lips. I kiss her long and slowly. To my surprise, she lets me. We get lost in each other. It is something I didn't know I needed. But I do, and based on the way she kisses me in return, she needs it too.

* * *

I keep waiting for the wave of grief to plow into me. To knock me down until I nearly drown.

It never comes.

I start to wonder if something might be wrong with me, but then I remember everything Tyler did. Every shit choice he made.

Instead, what I feel in place of sadness is relief. He can never hurt Finnley again. He can never hurt me or anyone else, for that matter, again.

I walk out of the hospital and spot Finnley sitting with Scott and Luke. Their backs are to me. They do not hear when I approach, Finnley's voice cracks and I halt. I swear to fuck, if they have upset her, I will lose it.

"I'm waiting for him to hate me."

Her words nearly knock the breath out of me. How can she possibly even think that?

I rush around to her and drop to my knees. Shock appears on her tear-streaked face. I grab her hands and squeeze tightly.

"Finnley, don't dare talk like that. I could never hate you. No way in hell. Understand?"

She smiles through her tears and my chest constricts.

"What I feel for you is the complete opposite of hate. I love you, Finnley. This does not change the way I feel."

"Awe, look at that, Brett has gone soft."

I shoot daggers at Scott. He puts his hands up in surrender. Fucker better watch it.

I stand up, pulling my girl with me. "Come on, let's go home."

"You're done? Already?"

I nod, pulling her along. I only had to come here to sign some papers. Seeing as I was Tyler's next of kin, I didn't have much choice. After signing, they asked which funeral home I wanted to use. I let out a sarcastic laugh and then told them to donate his body to a forensic science lab. The look on the poor guy's face was priceless. I walked away without so much as a glance back.

I don't care.

And I mean that.

No reason to have a viewing or service. Who

would come? My brother made more enemies than friends. The people he did call friends I doubt would even show up.

I open the passenger side door and help Finnley climb in. She looks at me and smiles.

"I never thanked you."

"Thanked me for what?" I question.

"For saving me."

I climb onto the running board and get right in her personal space. I reach for a curl that has fallen from her messy bun.

"I would do it again. As long as I get you, I would do it again."

"I know."

I smirk. "As long as you know." I kiss her lips once and jump down to go around to my side of the truck.

And I would.

I would go to the ends of the earth for her.

Chapter Thirty-Eight

Finnley

Weeks have passed since everything happened. Some days, it feels like eternity, others it as if it just happened. Some days, I am fine; other days, I break down.

All part of the healing process according to my therapist.

One thing that is mostly healed is my wounds. Only a few are still scabbed over. I had to take another round of antibiotics because one got infected. Other than that, I am good.

Scarred, but good.

I can live with that, I tell myself as I look myself over in the bathroom mirror. My stuff is littered all over the counter. One would never guess that I just recently moved in here.

I smile, pleased with my reflection. The olive-green see-through lace accents my pale skin and red hair. The teddy has a plunging neckline that makes my boobs look good. The lace does a good job of hiding my newly formed scars. Not that Brett would care.

He has been so gentle in my healing. Sometimes too gentle, like he is afraid he will break me.

And how I wish he would. I need him to break me. For him to break me and put me back together with his hands. His touch.

I have begged him so many times now. More times than I care to admit. Every time he gives me the same response. Some bullshit about needing to heal.

I get it. I think. Like I know I need to heal. It is just mentally I need him to be the one to control me. To tie me up. I want to surrender to him and his hands.

I finally told my therapist about my dilemma and Brett's reaction. She didn't judge me or make me feel like I was some sick individual. No, instead she told me that it is my way of trying to heal. She even suggested wearing something sexy to help Brett understand.

Well, tonight will be the night. I have already decided, and I refuse to take no for an answer.

I finish applying the candy apple red lipstick to my lips and cap it.

I walk out and take a seat on the chair in the

living room. It's angled toward the front door. I want to be the first thing Brett sees when he comes home from his shift. Just the thought has me squeezing my thighs shut. I need this. He needs this.

We need this.

It isn't long before I hear keys jingle. Excitement fills me.

Brett walks in and shuts the door behind him, locking it. When he turns around, his eyes land on me. The keys fall from his hand.

"Welcome home." I wink.

He's hot as hell in that uniform. Gray cargo pants and a black polo. I eye the holster around his waist.

Brett kneels and starts undoing the laces on his combat boots. The entire time, his eyes stay trained on me. His expression is serious, yet I can't quite tell if he is mad or not. Sometimes the man is hard to read, and this is one of those times.

As soon as he gets his boots off, he walks into the kitchen and washes his hands. Still, his eyes never leave me. I watch as they take in every inch of my body. From my pink-painted toes to my hair, Brett eyes me up and down.

"What is this?" he finally asks.

"Me for you to take."

Brett finishes in the kitchen and walks straight up to me. There is a tic in his perfectly chiseled jaw. A light line of stubble has started to grow back.

"Finnley?"

I don't bother to answer. Instead, I lean up, making sure to squeeze my breasts together. Reaching out, I grab his belt, making sure to run my palm over his erection. The second he stepped out from behind the counter, I noticed it. How could I not?

I pull him down to me. I kiss his neck, trailing up to just below his ear.

"I want you to cuff me. Cuff me and then fuck me," I whisper in his ears.

His body stiffens and I use the opportunity to grab him. He hisses in response before grabbing my wrist to still me.

"We can't."

"We can."

"You need to heal, baby. We have discussed this. A lot."

"I know. This is the last part of my healing journey," I say as I squeeze his erection before he can stop me.

"You're not ready."

"I have never been more ready. I need this. I need you to do this one thing for me. Please Brett." My voice cracks as it drops to a whisper. "Please take control. Cuff me and take control."

"Why do you want this so bad?"

"Because if someone is going to force control over me and my body, I want it to be you, not some creep who does it against my will. Please, help me erase what he did."

He lets out a long sigh while he chews on what I just admitted. It is not a lie.

"If I am going to be powerless, it is going to be to the man I love."

"Fuck, Finnley."

"Yes, let's fuck," I tease.

His cock twitches under my hand. A good sign, I hope. I squeeze him again before holding my hands out in front of me.

"Cuff me."

"I'm not sure this is healthy."

I shrug. "To the average person, it might not be considered healthy. To me, it is what I am craving."

He smirks and shakes his head at me. "What about after? What if you regret it or worse I end up reminding you of him?"

I have thought about this. I actually have even talked about it in therapy. At the end of the day, I choose this.

I grab his hand and pull it between my thighs. I let him feel how wet I am. His fingers toy with my clit. It feels like it has been forever since he has touched me. He circles slowly, and I must remember to focus.

"You could never remind me of him. Only you do this to me."

Brett swallows thickly before nodding his head slowly. He pulls his hand away from me, and I almost feel defeated.

That is until he pulls his hand cuffs out from his holster.

Chapter Thirty-Nine

Finnley

Brett pulls me up. He takes the cuffs and only puts them around one wrist before starting to walk me to the bedroom.

"What about the other wrist?"

"Patience, Finnley."

Well... okay then. His words come as a shock, but I will take it. I'll gladly take it.

Anticipation runs through my veins. We haven't had sex since the whole ordeal, and to be quite frank, I'm horny. Thoughts of what he is going to do swirl in my mind as excitement grows. I'm now soaked and can feel myself with each step we take.

Brett walks me over to the bed and gives me a gentle shove. I almost want to tell him that it is okay to be rough, but I don't want to push his buttons. I don't need him stopping now that we've started.

His hands glide up my legs and between my thighs. The second he inserts a finger, I relax, letting my head fall back. I have missed his touch more than he knows. As he finds a rhythm, I allow my eyes to drift close and to get lost in the moment. The need for him to touch me has been so strong that I promise myself to burn this into my memory.

A quiet moan escapes my lips when his fingers leave me. I pop my head up and open my eyes while I try to calm the panic that threatens to consume me.

"Brett?" I question. He can't back out of this. He can't be second guessing himself. I need this.

"Are you sure about this?"

"Never been surer of anything in my life."

And I haven't. Maybe I have gone off the deep end with this wild idea. Or maybe I just really want and need Brett to own my body. I want him to own me in the most delicious way. I just need to get him to see that.

Brett gives me a nod before reaching for my wrist. He brings it above my head and then grabs the other wrist. The one with the handcuff fastened around it.

He brings that hand above my head, bringing both hands together. I can feel him messing with the cuffs, and for some reason that excites me. Adrenaline starts pumping. I can't be sure, but I think he has pulled the cuff around the metal post of the bedframe.

The second cuff wraps around my boney wrist, but he does not close it.

"Finnley, are you sure you want me to cuff you?"

"Yes!" I spit out as that last word leaves his mouth.

"You will lose your power, control. You will have no control, do you really want that?"

"Yes, I want you to take my control. Take all of it." At this point, I sound like some crazed woman who is desperate for this. I mean, I am, but I have a good reason to sound like this.

The cuff clicks, and the room falls silent. Brett looks eerily calm. His eyes darken to something that can only be described as lust and desire. His eyes never leave mine. They are on me, studying, watching for any sign that I am about to regret this.

I'm not.

He comes down and kisses me. I open for him, allowing his tongues access. He pours every single emotion he is feeling into our kiss. I feel it all: the apprehension, the excitement. But most of all I feel his love.

And that is something that can only be felt. No words can describe it.

When he pulls back, his hands move to my

breasts, taking a nipple between his thumb and forefinger. When he pinches it slightly, I let out a moan.

"Finnley?" he questions, concern laced in his voice.

"Keep touching me. I need you to keep touching me. Erase his touch. Erase all of him from my body."

There is a tic in his jaw. He is chewing on my words, breaking down each one and what it exactly means.

Finally, he gives a slow nod. Probably to convince himself that I really am okay with this. He brings his mouth to my cheek. He trails light kisses along my jawline, down my neck, where he nips ever so lightly.

It feels so damn good.

His mouth moves down to my chest. He takes his time kissing me all over. It makes me wonder if he is working up the courage to keep going. Most likely, knowing him.

"Keep going," I whisper as I arch my chest up.

"Are you sure?"

"God, yes."

His mouth lands on my nipple, sucking on it through the lace. It's a tease yet feels so good with the fabric between us. While he is focusing on my nipple, his hand grazes my thigh, squeezing it. When he leans into me, I can feel his erection. On instinct, I go to move my hands so I can run my fingers through his hair and am reminded that I cannot do that. Fear fills me for a split second before euphoria takes over. It is almost blissful to relinquish all of myself to him.

Brett must feel me attempt to move my hands, he pauses and looks up at me.

"Do you want me to stop?" he asks as his hand slowly moves from my hip to my pussy.

"No."

That one word must satisfy him because his expression changes into what can only be described as a man starved.

His mouth crashes hard on my other breast. He sucks and nips with more force. At the same time, he inserts a finger into me. Once again, I can't do anything with my hands and that thought alone takes over. I have given Brett all control. It's almost freeing. I want him to take all of me.

Take it all, I tell myself.

Cool air hits my pebbled nipple. Brett stands back and removes his polo. Then he pulls me closer to the edge of the bed and pushes my thighs apart. Brett drops his head between them. As soon as I feel his tongue dart out against my clit, my eyes fall shut.

His tongue moves in wild motions. Absolutely zero rhythm. He is almost frantic. He is a man starved. He has not had me in weeks.

Every so often, without thinking, I try to pull my hands to him. I can't help it. The sensation of his mouth on me is too much, yet not enough. The light stubble along his jawline rubs against my thighs as I try to squeeze them shut.

Brett shoves them back open while continuing to feast. He groans in pleasure as his fingers dig into my thighs, pushing me closer to the edge.

"Please, more," I beg.

His moves slow, and it nearly drives me wild. Like I am about to lose control. He inserts a finger while his tongue swirls against my clit. I know he can feel me tightening around him. No doubt.

Brett picks up his pace again and his tongue moves just right. Flicking exactly where I need him to.

With my eyes squeezed shut, everything from the last few weeks fades away. All I feel is Brett and what he is doing to me. It's all I need to fall.

I fall. Hard.

I scream out his name as my orgasm reaches its peak. His tongue does not stop, nor does his finger as I come all over him. He laps me up like a man dehydrated.

"Brett!" I scream once more. The tingling sensation is too much. I squirm even though I am helpless to get away.

Brett finally gives me a reprieve and stands above me. I'm heaving deep breaths and for some reason I feel the threat of tears even though I couldn't be happier.

"Finnley, are you okay?"

He never fails to surprise me. Even though he just gave me one hell of an orgasm, he is still concerned about me wanting to go through with this.

I nod, afraid that if I speak, the dam of tears will break.

"You're not fine. You're about to cry. You regret this?"

"No! No, not at all." I feel a single tear fall. Dammit.

"You do, you are crying."

"Happy tears."

"Happy tears?" he questions, a crease furrowed between his eyebrows.

"Yes, happy tears. Come kiss me."

He does as I ask, kissing me softly at first. He may not realize it yet, but he just fixed a part of me. He is putting my damaged pieces back together.

"I love you," I whisper against his lips.

A growl practically leaves his mouth as he repeats the words to me. He stands and removes the rest of his clothes.

"I am going to remove the cuffs and then I am going to fuck you."

"No!" I say fast. "Don't take them off."

"Finnley, I am removing them. I did what you

wanted. Now, I want you to take whatever you need from me. I will not be taking no for an answer? Do you understand that?"

Giving in, I nod. "Yes."

I hear him loud and clear.

Chapter Forty

Brett

As soon as Finnley speaks the word, my restraint folds. I undress. I had refrained from undressing earlier. I did not want to be fully naked if she changed her mind.

I should have known she wouldn't back down. She has only been begging me for this. I just hope she has no regrets after.

I pull the cuffs completely off and toss them aside. I push her thighs apart as I climb over her. Her pussy is glistening. I did that to her. Something like pride swells in my chest as dominance takes over.

Finnley Thompson is mine.

My cock throbs as I line it up at her entrance. My eyes leave where we are about to be joined and I look at her to get confirmation that she wants me to continue.

Fuck, I hope she wants me to continue but understand if she doesn't.

Beautiful green eyes stare back at me with such desire that I can hardly wait another second. I nudge slowly.

"Are you sure you want this?" I ask.

Instead of an answer, Finnley brings her arms around, grasping my ass. Her nails dig into my flesh as she urges me in. My cock slides right in with how wet she is. And fuck me, she feels so good.

I have missed this connection with her. To be one.

I try to move slowly at first, wanting to savor our intimate moments. She, on the other hand, has other plans. She lifts her hips to try to get me to move faster.

"We have all the time in the world." I lean to kiss her.

"I don't want soft, I want it hard and fast." She pouts while continuing to move her hips.

"Please, Brett, please."

Her words do something to me. I grow possessive, alpha. I want to own and worship her body at the same time.

I reach under her ass and arch her up. Hitting her deep and at just the right angle. My movements are no longer slow. Finnley cries out in pleasure while grasping and scratching my thighs.

"Last time, are you sure you still want this?"

"God, yes!" she pants.

My movements grow rough, hard. It doesn't take long before her hips buck and she starts to go wild. Each thrust has me closer to exploding inside of her, yet I push the thoughts away. Not yet.

I lean in close to her ear and all but growl, "I will do anything to erase that sick fuck from your mind. Anything. I will fuck your brains out until he is nothing more."

"Yes! Brett, Yes!" she moans before taking her hard nipples between her fingers.

Fuck. Seeing her touch herself drives me fucking insane. I thrust harder even though I know she will be bruised and sore by the time I am done with her.

As long as it is me marking her, no one else, that is all that matters. No one else gets that right.

"Brett!" Finnley screams out as her pussy clamps around my dick.

"That's it. Come undone."

Her orgasm hits her hard. Hearing her incoherent words as her hands lash out at me. Marking me in the same way I am marking her. I revel in the pain that mixes with pleasure.

It's too much, yet not enough.

I fucking explode inside of her. Her screams turn to whimpers while I continue with hard, deep thrusts filling every inch of her with my cum.

I roll us both until she is lying on top of me

with my cock still inside of her. I push the hair out of her face as she lays her head on my chest. Warmth spreads throughout me. She fits perfectly. A feeling of calm has washed over me and I hope like hell I was able to give her exactly what she wanted.

"Finnley," I say, not wanting to break the silence, but knowing I need to. "Are you okay?"

"Never been better," she croaks. Her throat is probably going raw from shouting out my name among other things.

"Did I give you what you wanted? Did I erase that fucker?"

"Mmhm."

Do you feel at peace?"

Finnley lifts her head. My now placid cock threatens to fall out of her pussy. She sits up further to adjust herself, keeping me inside of her. Her perky tits are now on display for me and me only. They cause my cock to twitch.

"Yes. I am at peace. You bring me a sense of peace I have never known." She leans down and places a kiss on my forehead.

My eyes go to the lace that barely covers the newly formed scars. I reach out slowly, tracing them.

"I will heal each and every one of these."

"I know you will. You already started the healing process, more than you know."

Pride beams in my soul at her words. If I could puff out my chest and beat my fists, I would. Instead I snake my arms around her back side and rub little circles on her lower back while mindlessly grabbing her ass. When I do, she sits back on my cock further, fully seating herself.

Fuck. Her pussy feels good.

She feels good.

Finnley begins to ride me with slow and deliberate movements. Movements that feel so good they could kill a man.

Her steady movements have me rock hard in no time. Once she finds her rhythm, tiny whimpers leave her lips. I help by lifting her ass each time she bounces on my cock. I watch where our bodies meet. Both of our juices mix as one.

We are one.

This is how it should be.

She rides me harder, her tits bouncing as she does. I feel her tightening around my cock once more, telling me she is close. Reaching down, I rub her swollen clit until she breaks.

Finnley screams out my name, and I briefly wonder if my neighbors can hear her screams.

I hope fucking so. Let them hear who this fiery redhead belongs to.

This time, when she comes back down to earth, she falls to my chest, and I know she has no more energy left. I slow my moments, not caring if I finish this round. I won't take more than she can give.

I refuse.

"Brett," she whispers, her hot breath beats across my chest.

"Baby."

"Thank you."

"For what?"

"For not seeing me as a broken woman."

I kiss the top of her head and think back over the last few weeks and how I would not so much as touch her. I wouldn't let her touch me. I was worried.

"You are fucking amazing. You hear me? You have blown me away with your ability to persevere."

Finnley lifts her head slightly at me and smiles.

"I told you, I'm not broken."

She sure did. She sure fucking did.

Playlist

I'm constantly listening to music while plotting, writing, and editing. Below are a few songs I listened to while creating Finnley & Brett's story. You can enjoy the full playlist for Not Broken here:
Not Broken on Spotify

Close- Nick Jonas & Tove Lo
Dancing With A Stranger - Sam Smith & Normani
Broken- Lovelytheband
I Don't Want This Night To End- Luke Bryan
Middle Of The Night- Elley Duhé
Fix You- Coldplay
Darkness Settles In- Five Finger Death Punch

To stay up with the latest happenings, please sign up for my newsletter, or join my reader group.

Xoxo,
Lisamarie

Newsletter

Lisamarie's Romance Readers

Acknowledgments

First and always, to my readers: Thank you. Thank you for supporting an indie-author.

To Erin: Thank you for always supporting me. For going along with my book ideas and supporting me every step of the way.

To my Romance Babes: Thank you for your support. I love our reader group.

To Beth: Thank for not only being my editor, but also my friend.

To my husband: Thank you for being my biggest cheerleader.

About the Author

Hi there! By now, you probably know my name, Lisamarie Kade. I write erotic romance. My books range from steamy to extra spicy. Most of my books contain secrets and a lot of sex!

I'm a lover of reading, coffee, Reese Cups, good music- especially emo, all things hot pink, and candles that smell like sexy men.

When not writing, you can find me spending time with my husband and our small army of children. Most days I can be seen looking like a hot mess while taking the kids to one of their many activities.

Also by Lisamarie Kade

The Secrets We Keep

Mended Hearts

The Christmas Breakdown

The War Within

The Surprise Within

Shattered Illusion

Shattered Reality

A Little Winter Romance

A Little Winter Fling